Four Month Friend

by Susan Clymer

Illustrated by
Sandy Rabinowitz

Scholastic Inc.

New York

Library of Congress Cataloging-in-Publication Data
Clymer, Susan.
    Four month friend / by Susan Clymer; illustrated by Sandy Rabinowitz.
      p.   cm.
    Summary: Staying with her uncle on his California farm, nine-year-old
Dani feels unwelcome and unloved while she tries to come up with a plan to
save her pet goat Tyler from the butcher.
    ISBN 0-590-42544-7
    [1. Goats—Fiction.   2. Farm life—Fiction.   3. Uncles—Fiction.]
I. Rabinowitz, Sandy, ill.   II. Title.
PZ7.C62726Fo   1990
[Fic]—dc20

                                           89-10618
                                              CIP
                                              AC

12 11 10 9 8 7 6 5 4 3 2 1   0 1 2 3 4 5/9

Printed in the U.S.A.   37

First Scholastic printing, March 1990

Design by Tracy Arnold

For Laura Reed Ashley
with love
and great thanks for your support
of my dreams. . . .
This book is truly yours.

1 A Sharp Fierce Cry

Dani crouched against the corner of the tiny shed. The goat lay in the opposite corner, only as far away as the length of Dani's body. The goat's breathing had grown harder and faster. Now she bleated, a sharp fierce cry. The sound made Dani want to jump to her feet and run from the barn, then climb the highest tree she could find. Yet Dani knew she shouldn't run. The baby goat might be born soon.

Uncle Walter had said that sometimes animals needed help with their first babies. Someone should be with Jen when this first kid was born. No one was home but her.

The goat bleated again, louder this time. Dani clamped both hands over her ears and closed one eye. The goat pushed against the rough wooden wall of the barn with her back legs. Something was coming out of her. It looked like a bubble. No, it was a hoof . . . two hoofs. That must mean the

1

baby was being born frontward, the right way!

Then the movement stopped.

Come on, little baby. Be born! Dani urged silently. Uncle Walter had said last night that sometimes a first kid would get stuck while being born. Then a person had to pull gently on the tiny hoofs toward the doe's back. Dani pressed herself up against the wall of the barn so hard that she could feel the wood digging into her shoulder blades. She was supposed to pull on those hoofs? She couldn't! Yet the hoofs still weren't moving. If she didn't help, the baby might die.

Careful not to make the tiniest sound, Dani crawled toward Jen. Suddenly the goat took two giant breaths and pushed again. Dani froze on her knees and one hand, so close she could have reached out and touched the mother goat's back. The hoofs were moving again. There was the baby's nose! And the head! Then with a swoosh the whole body was out.

Dani's elbow almost collapsed beneath her, and she felt like cheering. Hurray! HURRAY! she thought.

She could hardly see what the tiny goat

looked like through that slimy white stuff that covered its body. Dani sat back. All Jen had to do now was to lick the white stuff off her baby's nose and mouth so it could breath.

The seconds passed, and the mother goat just lay there. Her brown sides heaved up and down.

"Jen!" Dani whispered, but the mother goat didn't move. The kid would die if it didn't get any air. Frantically, Dani counted. "One ... two ..." If Jen didn't start licking by the count of ten, she would have to help. Why couldn't Uncle Walter or even cousin Clorissa be home? Dani felt the sweat prickling out on the palms of her hands, and her stomach moved as though she'd swallowed a live crab. "... nine ... ten."

Dani yanked down the damp clean cloth she had brought from the house and crawled toward the baby goat. She was afraid to even touch the baby. Cautiously, Dani reached out with the towel and dabbed at the stuff around the kid's mouth and nose. It was stickier than spit. Dani barely kept herself from groaning aloud.

Then, through the white film, she noticed

that the kid had the same white stripe down its muzzle as Jen. Oh, she couldn't let the baby die! Dani held the kid's head in her left hand. The newborn goat felt warm, slippery. Dani wiped the face as firmly as she could.

The baby made a half-strangled gasping sound. Dani almost let go of its head as she gasped, too. The mother goat shifted her body around. She knocked Dani's hand roughly away and started licking at her baby's mouth and nose. The kid breathed again and again.

"You're alive!" Dani exclaimed. "You're alive!" She forgot to be quiet. "I helped you be born!" Jen licked at the kid's shoulders and belly, and Dani leaned closer. It was a boy goat.

"Tyler," Dani whispered. That's what she would name him. Tyler. Five minutes ago, Jen had been the only goat. Now there was this new baby lying stretched out on the ground. From front hoofs to back hoofs, the kid measured about as long as Dani's arm. Yet someday he would grow to be as big as Jen. The little goat moved. He was already trying to lift his head. Maybe he would do tricks when he grew up, like in a circus. Tyler, the acrobat.

"You here alone?" a gruff voice asked. Uncle Walter tiptoed into the barn. It was hard to imagine a big man like Uncle Walter tiptoeing.

"Uncle Walter!" Dani grabbed his pants leg in her excitement. "I helped . . ."

Uncle Walter lifted his finger to his mouth for silence and nodded at the rag in her hand. "Good." Then he pointed to the barn door. "Go on to the house, now. There will be another baby coming along soon. You've seen enough."

Dani stared at him. Go?!

"Out," he said firmly.

Dani stumbled to the door, shocked back into silence. Uncle Walter took the rag from her as she passed.

Outside, the sun lay low in the sky, almost resting on the horizon. She must have been in the barn for hours since coming home from school. Dani stretched her shoulders, then glared at the shed. She deserved to watch the rest of the birthing. How could Uncle Walter make her leave? Tyler wouldn't even be alive without her.

Dani climbed over the railing on the front porch of the house and dropped into Uncle Walter's rocking chair. Every day Uncle Walter drove all over the county for his job fixing copying machines. Every evening he painted pictures in his artist's studio in the basement. Before he started painting, he would sit here in this chair and rock. He said it helped him think. Dani rocked. She wished her mom were here. Mom would be proud of her helping the baby goat, even if Uncle Walter wasn't. Dani rocked harder. Mom wouldn't be here for nine more months and twelve days according to the calendar Dani had hanging in her cubbyhole in the attic.

Mom had won a special scholarship to study in Oxford, England, for a year. Dad always traveled a lot. So her parents had brought Dani to California to be with Uncle Walter and cousin Clorissa. Alone.

Dani still couldn't believe Mom had left her. She had taken her away from their little cottage in Portland, Oregon, and *all* of her friends . . . and dropped her here, in the middle of nowhere, away from the ocean and the seabirds.

Dani heard Jen crying aloud again. Her bleats sounded terrible. The second kid must be being born. Dani put her hands over her ears and wondered if Tyler was afraid of his mother's cries.

"What are you doing, pest?" Clorissa

came down the path from the junior high bus. She held her books in the crook of one arm and walked with an easy swaying motion. How could she still look so neat after a whole day of school? By the time Dani got home every day she looked as if she'd been in the middle of a whirlwind of ink or mud.

"The goats are being born," Dani answered. She hated being called a pest, but arguing with Clorissa never did any good.

"Ooooohhhh." Clorissa's voice started way up high, then slid down. She seemed impressed. Clorissa put her books down side by side on the porch, wiped them off, then sat on them. She stretched her light blue skirt over her knees. The sounds from the shed stopped.

"I helped the first baby being born, Clorissa," Dani said. "I named him Tyler."

Clorissa looked at her strangely, with that I-am-older-and-know-better-than-you look. "Dani, a male goat? You shouldn't . . ."

Uncle Walter stuck his head out of the barn. "Come on in and see them, you two. They are mighty nice-looking." Dani stood up and swung her feet over the porch railing, landing with a thump on the ground. She wanted to know what Clorissa had been about to say, but she wanted to see the goats more. Dani zipped across the yard, then made herself walk quietly into the barn so she wouldn't disturb Jen. She didn't want to give Uncle Walter an excuse to make her leave again, either.

Another new baby goat lay stretched out by Jen's head. Tyler was trying to get his front legs under his body to stand up, but he fell onto his nose. His hair had fluffed out, like a rabbit's fur. He didn't look slimy at all. Tyler's body was chocolate brown, but he had white legs from the knees down and a strip of white on his muzzle. The outside of his ears looked like they had been covered with blobs of white snow.

Dani grinned proudly as the tiny goat tried to stand again. He was already trying to do a trick. Tyler must be the best goat in the whole world. And *she* had helped him be born.

2 Sold for Meat?

The next morning Dani awakened to see sunlight shining through the attic window. The light danced across the sea gull on her nightshirt. Still half asleep, Dani imagined Tyler with his wobbly little legs trying to run along the ground after a sea gull . . . the way the dogs did at home in Portland.

Thinking about Tyler reminded her that she had a special question to ask Uncle Walter. Dani rolled out of bed, careful not to hit her head on the slanting eaves. Her uncle would be awake by now, doing his chores.

First, Dani crossed off a day on her homemade calendar, the way she did every morning. Counting today there were nine months and eleven days until Mom came home. Dani raced down the wooden stairs two at a time, buttoning her shirt as she ran.

"Keep quiet, *elephant!*" Clorissa yelled from her room.

Startled, Dani caught hold of the banister to stop herself. "Sorry," she called. She hadn't meant to wake up Clorissa. Her cousin loved to sleep late on the weekends. Dani tiptoed down the stairs. Yet by the time she reached the bottom, her face felt fiery hot. She was *not* an elephant. She was not a pest, either. Dani jumped on the landing with both feet . . . as hard as she could. Then she dashed outside and slammed the front door behind her.

Every time Dani left the house, she turned a cartwheel across the porch. This morning she barely lifted her legs into the air, but she didn't go back to make the cartwheel perfect. She couldn't wait to see the goats.

Tyler stood in front of the small shed with his mother and his sister. Uncle Walter had named the other baby Willy. She had a tan coat. Together, Tyler and Willy looked like a double-decker cookie, one chocolate and one vanilla. Both babies had tiny fluffy ears that stuck straight up. When they saw Dani running, they staggered away side by side toward the barn.

"Come on out, Tyler," Dani sang softly. Perhaps the little goats wouldn't be afraid of her if she were more their size. Dani got down on her hands and knees to peer around the edge of the barn door. Only a few inches away, she saw Tyler's face. He had a yellow stripe across the middle of each eye. "Baaa," Dani said. Tyler fell backward in surprise. He was such a baby.

"Better watch it. Your bottom is about to be used for target practice," Uncle Walter called.

Dani ducked out of the barn. Sure enough, Jen had lowered her head, aiming right at Dani's seat. The mother goat was protecting her babies. Dani didn't want to be butted, even if Toggenburg goats didn't have horns. She scrambled out of the way and came up on her feet.

Uncle Walter leaned against his shovel. He wore his normal weekend outfit of overalls and T-shirt, brown sandals and a hat. He did most of his farm work on Saturdays, weeding in the vegetable garden and taking care of the animals.

"Uncle Walter?" Dani asked. Now she would get to ask the question she'd been thinking about all night long. "Can I keep Tyler? Can he be my goat?"

Uncle Walter looked at the ground. "Well . . ." he began.

"Please! I'm going to be here for so long." Dani grabbed hold of the shovel right beneath her uncle's hand. Uncle Walter didn't seem to like to be touched the way her parents did.

Still Uncle Walter hesitated.

"Dad can't give you the goat, *elephant*!" Clorissa exclaimed from the porch.

Dani twisted around. Clorissa wore her pink robe and tennis shoes. Her hair stuck straight up in the back. Uh-oh. She never came out of her bedroom without her hair combed.

She must still be mad about being awakened. Or maybe she was upset because Uncle Walter had told her last night that she had to come straight home from school from now on to be with Dani. No more late bus. That meant no more drill team for Clorissa or even coed volleyball on Wednesdays. Uncle Walter thought Dani was too young to handle things around here alone . . . like Jen's having babies.

"Tyler's a male goat, pest," Clorissa said nastily. She stomped across the yard toward Dani. "He will be sold for meat."

"Clorissa," Uncle Walter said in a warning voice.

"Meat?" Dani didn't understand. Her

arms prickled into goose bumps.

"He will be sold in a butcher shop while he's still tender," Clorissa continued, her voice almost singsong. "Someone will eat him."

Uncle Walter turned faster than Dani had ever seen him move. He grabbed his daughter by the shoulder. Instantly, Clorissa fell silent, her eyes as giant as the baby goats'.

Dani's throat tightened. "Someone will eat Tyler?" she cried. For a moment Dani imagined Tyler hanging from a hook in a butcher's shop by his front hoofs . . . those same hoofs that she'd almost had to pull on yesterday to help him be born. Dani didn't think she had screamed, but both Uncle Walter and Clorissa backed away.

Uncle Walter spoke gently. "I have to sell the goat before he is four months old." He glared at Clorissa. "You could have told her nicer. What's the matter with you?"

Dani pulled on Uncle Walter's shirt. "You can't sell Tyler!"

"Male goats smell when they get big," Clorissa said more softly. "They make the milk from the females smell, too." She scrunched up her nose and held it with two fingers while pretending to hold a glass with her other hand.

"Awful." Uncle Walter's face crinkled. "So bad you can't even drink it. So, when they get to be four months old, the males here are sold for meat. Dani, you need to understand that this farm is a business. We don't ever keep extra mouths to feed."

Dani stumbled backward. Were they making fun of killing a little goat? Even Uncle Walter? She drew her hands into fists, so furious that she wanted to make them mad, too. The only way Dani had ever been able to make her mother really angry was to speak incorrect English. "I ain't gonna let you kill Tyler," Dani yelled right at Uncle Walter's face. "You couldn't never find a better goat!" She folded her arms across her chest and waited.

Clorissa giggled and reached out with one hand. "You get your language all wrong when you're mad, pest."

"Easy," Uncle Walter mumbled. "She's upset." He smiled at Dani, a half-lopsided smile that with his straw hat made him look like a clown.

He wasn't even mad! Uncle Walter didn't care if she didn't speak correctly. Dani stared at him, at his hands that must be three times the size of hers. He didn't care about her at all! With a sob, Dani turned and ran.

"Dani!" Uncle Walter called.

She ignored him. She kept running to the back fence. Dani climbed the nearby tree, shinnied along a limb, and dropped to the other side of the fence. Alone, she leaned her head against a tree. Then she pretended the tree was her mother. "Mom, they're going to sell Tyler for meat when he gets big just because he will smell. People will eat him!!"

The tree didn't answer. Dani kicked at the trunk and rubbed the back of her hand across her eyes. She would never last over nine months until her mother came back. She couldn't stand it here.

Dani moved toward the target she had set up in the back lot and threw the pile of old tennis balls one by one. All she had done for the last three months was come home from school and read. She was tired of reading! She wanted somebody to be friends with her. Her best friend from home had only written once in three months.

Tyler would be her friend.

For a moment, Dani's eyes blurred so badly that she could hardly see the target.

At least Tyler would have been her friend if they weren't going to take him away. Dani threw another ball, hard. She couldn't even play baseball here in the country, in the middle of nowhere. If she were at home in Portland, she would have joined a team for the first time.

Dani dropped the ball. Baseball wasn't important now. Slowly, Dani climbed back over the fence and walked toward the barn, scuffling her feet in the weeds. She and Uncle Walter and Clorissa had always gotten along before she had come to live here. Now it seemed like everything she did was wrong. She was always an elephant or making so much noise that Uncle Walter couldn't concentrate on his painting. Her uncle never read books to her like Mom or took her for walks to watch birds like her father. All he did was work and paint. Dani leaned against a tree, one arm around its trunk. No one even hugged each other here.

From where Dani stood, she could see every corner of the little farm. She could see the chicken coop, the vegetable garden, the field of grass behind the house . . . and the goat shed.

Tyler and Willy stood outside the shed again, right next to their mother. Dani tiptoed close and sat down to watch. Tyler wouldn't be killed for four months. Four whole months.

Uncle Walter came out of the chicken coop and walked by her with a bowl of eggs in his hand. He was staring off into space. He probably hadn't seen her.

"Uncle Walter?" Dani's voice came out a whisper.

The big man didn't say anything, but he stopped, and his eyes came into focus.

Dani spoke louder. "Can Tyler be mine until he's four months old?"

Uncle Walter nodded. In fact, he really looked at her.

"Then I can try to find Tyler a home," Dani said hopefully. To her embarrassment, her voice rose. "Some people like male goats, right?"

"Dani, there's a market for young male goats," Uncle Walter said. "I can use that money."

Dani swallowed. "Money?!" First, her uncle had said he'd let Tyler be destroyed because he smelled, now he said he'd do it for money. "Keep my allowance then!"

This time she knew she had screamed.

"Dani." Uncle Walter sounded as if he wished he could ship her back to Portland. He sighed. "All right, you can try to find him a home." He walked to the edge of the porch, then hesitated. "Don't get too attached. Four months will come up real soon."

Dani watched her uncle as he disappeared into the house. She wished he would smile more, just a little. She turned toward the shed.

Tyler walked under Jen and butted at her udder with his tiny head. He lifted his muzzle to suckle. Jen's milk must be warm. Tyler's stubby tail wagged as he drank. Then he wobbled closer to where Dani sat. He stood still, his little legs stretched out wide in front and behind him for balance.

Dani didn't move. Slowly, she reached out her hand. The chocolate brown goat bolted away, but he staggered and fell on his nose. Awkwardly, he stood up again, then hopped toward her. At least it was almost a hop. Dani smiled. Tyler liked her, even if no one else here did. He would be her friend, her best friend. For four months.

3 Follow the Leader

Dani crept down the stairs in the early morning light. Every morning at six o'clock and every evening at six she milked the mother goat. She hadn't missed a single day in the three weeks since Tyler and Willy had been born. Milking was a thousand times better than doing the dishes like Clorissa. Besides, learning to set an alarm clock and get up by herself seemed adventurous . . . sometimes even spooky.

Dani flipped her baseball cap off the hook by the door, and a white envelope fluttered to the ground. A letter! Uncle Walter must have gone to the post office last night after she had gone to bed. He had put the letter right where he knew she would find it.

Mom hadn't written for five days. Usually, she wrote every two or three days. Dani ripped off the end of the envelope, her heart thumping. A picture slipped halfway out. The first thing Dani saw was her mother smiling. Dani tugged the photograph loose. Mom stood on the back of a boat that looked a bit like a flat canoe. She held a long, thin pole and was pushing the boat along. Dani grinned. Her mom's pants and blouse looked wet. She'd fallen in the water.

Beside the boat floated a beautiful white bird, the biggest Dani had ever seen. The bird looked bigger than a duck or a goose. It must be a swan!

Dani wished she could see a swan in real life, not just in a picture. Dani sat down hard on the bottom step. She wanted to see her mother, too. She missed her so much. Mom, Dani thought for the millionth time, why did you have to go . . . when you couldn't take me?!

When the news of the scholarship had first come, her mother had wrapped Dani in her arms and explained that going to study in Oxford had been a dream she'd had all her life. Mom said she had to go.

Dani sighed and twisted the letter so there would be enough light on the page to read.

Dear Danielle,

I know how much you love green, so I decided to write this letter in green ink.

Remember last year when we read *Alice in Wonderland* aloud together? The author of the book, Lewis Carroll, lived here in Oxford over a hundred years ago. One day, Mr. Carroll went boating on the Thames (That's the river in your picture!) with three girls who were sisters. One of the girl's names was Alice. As they floated along the river, Lewis Carroll made up a story about Alice having adventures in an imaginary world called Wonderland. At the end of the day, Alice begged him to write the story down. So . . . *Alice in Wonderland* was first created on the river in your photograph, darling.

Love,
Mom

P.S. The swan in this picture belongs to the Queen of England. All the swans on the River Thames belong to the Queen.

P.P.S. I send 100 kisses!!!!!!!!!!!!!!

Gently, Dani wrapped the picture in the letter. She would go to the library this very afternoon. As she read *Alice in Wonderland,* she would imagine that she was rowing down the River Thames with a big white swan floating by. Dani put the letter in her pocket. Her mother must love her. She had called her darling and sent 100 kisses.

Dani put her baseball cap in her teeth and zipped her sweatshirt up to her neck before stepping into the chilly, shadowy morning. As usual, she turned a cartwheel along the porch, an almost perfect one this time. Then Dani pulled on her cap, shivering. She imagined her mother hugging her and kissing her on the cheek. Ninety-nine more kisses would last a long time.

Dani stood still to watch the goats and listen to the dawn sounds. The birds had begun to awaken. She could even hear a morning dove. The sun had barely poked its head up over the horizon. Jen stood outside the shed, happily ripping the bark off the oak tree. Uncle Walter wouldn't like that.

Willy and Tyler leaped at each other inside the doorway of the shed and clunked their little heads together.

Maybe today would be a special day, because she'd gotten a letter from Mom. Dani took a deep breath. Maybe she should try the first step of her new plan for Tyler, Plan T. Tyler had needed her when he was born. But Dani knew he needed her even more now. Without her help, he might be eaten by strange people for dinner. Dani shook her head to get rid of the horrible thought.

First, she had to milk Jen. Then she could try her new plan. Dani sneaked to the side of the shadowy barn, and pushed the door shut so the babies would be stuck inside. Jen took a flying leap and slid eagerly onto the milking stand. Dani circled a teat with her thumb and first finger and then rolled her other fingers down one by one. She only got a tiny squirt of milk in the bucket. The damp coolness of the early morning made her hands work more slowly than usual. Milking a goat was *hard*.

Finally, Dani unlatched the shed door, the half-full bucket in her hand. "Hey, kids!"

The wailing babies came out in a rush. Tyler dashed to take a quick suckle of milk from his mother, then raced up the big plank that Uncle Walter had leaned against the shed for the goats to get exercise. Willy stayed with Jen, suckling. Dani tried to pat Tyler as he passed her shoulder. She missed. This time, Tyler climbed from the plank onto the steep roof of the shed. He trotted up to the very top, then balanced on the narrow ridge with all four hoofs together. His little spotted ears lay back against his head. All Dani could see behind him was the sky. She wished she had a camera.

Dani knew that goats by nature liked to climb. Tyler sure did. Uncle Walter had said that he was the climbingest goat he'd ever seen.

Dani entered the shed and poured the milk through a strainer into a clean jar. She could hear Tyler's feet clattering on the roof above her like hail. Now would be the time to try the first step in Plan T.

Grabbing a handful of fresh hay, Dani touched her mother's letter for luck. She stepped back outside. Tyler was sliding down the plank onto the ground.

"Hey, Tyler. Look!" Dani called.

The kid ignored her. Dani waved the hay right in front of his face. He was supposed to be interested!

Tyler leaped into the wheelbarrow. Then

he sprang out stiff-legged as the barrow tipped over, and he ambled away from Dani and the hay, bored.

Luckily, Dani had already thought of a backup idea for the first step in Plan T. She zipped inside the house and climbed up on the counter to get the jar of molasses. She liked molasses. Maybe Tyler would, too. But she had to hurry! She could already hear Uncle Walter and Clorissa getting up. Dani wiped her footprints off the counter with her sleeve.

Outside again, she poured molasses over a bunch of hay. She waved the sticky mass

in front of Tyler's nose. He sniffed and nibbled. Dani gave Tyler another bite, then moved away a few steps. "Tyler!" Dani waved the hay. She held her breath, hoping.

This time the chocolate brown goat looked when she called his name. He bounded closer, his little spotted ears rising straight up. He landed with his front hoofs right together, then playfully dropped his head as if he were going to race forward and butt her.

Come to me, little friend, Dani thought as hard as she could. "Tyler!!"

The little goat bounded toward her again. Who said a goat wouldn't come to his name? Slowly, Dani backed up, waving the hay and calling him. Every few steps she gave him little bits of hay to munch.

Tyler was following her away from his mother! Dani wanted to turn handsprings across the lawn. Uncle Walter had explained to her that goats instinctively followed other goats, that they liked to be in a herd. That's how she'd gotten this big idea to teach Tyler to follow her . . . to consider her the leader.

She planned to teach him to go on walks

with her, so that when he got older she could take him visiting. She would show him to all the farmers, even the people near town with regular backyards. Some family would want to buy the little goat for a pet after they had seen how many tricks he could do. Having Tyler would be like having their own private acrobat. Dani leaned down to hug him. Tyler chewed happily on the collar of her school shirt. Then he bleated and ran back to his mother.

Dani walked on her hands for almost three steps on her way to the barn to get the fresh goat milk for breakfast. Already this was a special day. Plan T, short for Tyler tricks, might work! On a morning like this, she could even stand to eat Uncle Walter's sticky boring oatmeal. She would pretend to be eating pancakes and wild blackberry ice cream from Portland . . . while floating on the River Thames with Tyler and her mother.

4 Dani's Discovery

Never before had Dani been alone in Uncle Walter's private artist's studio in the basement of the farmhouse. Her uncle had come home early today and taken Jen and the month-old babies to the vet for shots and a checkup. So, Dani had decided to be an explorer.

She tiptoed under Uncle Walter's new charcoal drawing of a pig with big ears. The pig seemed to be staring right at her from the drawing, listening with those giant ears. Dani giggled, then covered her mouth so Clorissa, talking upstairs on the phone in the kitchen, wouldn't hear. Silently, Dani skirted a pile of canvases and stopped in front of an unfinished picture resting on the easel by the window. Was this what Uncle Walter was working on right now? Fascinated, Dani reached out to touch the green tree.

Her finger stuck to the damp paint.

Dani yanked her hand away. Oh, no! Green paint stuck to her fingertip, and tiny swirl marks remained on the painted tree. Uncle Walter wouldn't notice one little fingerprint, would he?

All her uncle's oil paints lay scattered over the table next to the easel. A green tube of paint rested against a blue one. The red and yellow tubes were in a little pile. What a mess!

Uncle Walter wouldn't mind if she helped him clean, even if she was supposed to be a secret explorer. Dani started by shifting the four shades of green into a neat row along the top of the table.

The purples reminded her of her classroom baseball team, the Purple Panthers. Today, they had beaten Ms. Andel's class, the Yellow Jackets. Dani had been the pitcher. If her class won next week, they'd be champions of the whole grade.

Dani arranged the yellows and reds into two lines, then the blues. The tubes felt squishy, but firm. Dani wanted to take off the tops. She could make a fabulous picture without even using a paintbrush.

But she didn't dare.

She'd been here long enough. If Clorissa caught her, she'd be in deep trouble. She crept past the wall covered with drawings of the countryside. Dani halted beside Uncle

31

Walter's new sketchbook. She peeked at the top picture, a drawing of their shed.

With a sigh, Dani closed the book. Clorissa had explained that Uncle Walter never shared what he was working on right now. So looking at these pictures would be like reading a private diary . . . tempting, but not fair.

Just then, Clorissa hung up the phone with a bang. Dani sprinted up the stairs. She sneaked past the kitchen door. "I'm going exploring!" she yelled.

She heard her cousin laugh. "Try the deep, dark snake-ridden forest, pest."

That remark made Dani forget her usual cartwheel along the front porch. No one in Oregon called her names. Dani headed up the driveway, suddenly homesick. She had eight months and twelve days before she'd see her friends or her home again.

Still, Clorissa had given her an idea. She could explore the woods she passed walking home from the bus each day. Dani climbed over the low stone wall that ran alongside the road. She crossed the little stream, carefully balancing on rocks. Snakes really could live in these woods. Dani counted her steps into the forest. On twelve, she found a path. What luck!

As Dani stalked along the path, she imagined animals hiding behind the bushes. Some of them would be friendly and some vicious. She imagined bravely meeting an animal that was half tiger and half whale, a tigale. The front half liked living on land and the back half adored water.

The path branched. Dani chose the right-hand path. From the top of a little hill, she could see a fence. The fence surrounded a yard with a beaten-down circle in the middle, like a track. Then Dani noticed stables. A horse farm!

She raced down the hillside toward the horses. She'd always wanted to learn how to ride. People sometimes rode horses on the beaches in Oregon. Dani crawled under the fence into the yard. She'd never even touched a horse.

Dani was still on her hands and knees when she heard something rushing toward her, growling fiercely. Dani looked up at a giant dog. She didn't have time to crawl back under the fence, so she stood up. Her heart thumped. She could see the German shepherd's teeth as it raced closer. Dani swallowed, holding out her hand in a fist the way her mother had taught her. That dog must weigh more than she did. "Good dog." Her words sounded strangled.

Two feet away, the dog stopped. Her ruff stuck out around her neck. Dani knew better than to move. This was a guard dog, trained not to allow anyone on its property. The dog barked.

"Her name's Nellie," a man said dryly. "Scares off most people."

Dani glanced behind her. She saw a skinny man with a black cap on his head . . . a cap like Dad's!

Now that the man had come, Dani figured the dog wouldn't be dangerous. She held out both hands. "Nellie." Her voice shook a bit. "Come here, Nellie!"

The shepherd sat down.

Dani crouched. "Good girl, Nellie." The dog thumped her tail and looked at her owner with a whine.

The man stepped closer. "Need my permission, do you?" He waved one hand in what looked like a signal. "Make friends."

The dog bounded over to Dani. She licked her from her chin to the top of her head.

"Yuck!" Dani exclaimed, but she didn't really mind. She wiped her face off with her sleeve. The dog turned abruptly and trotted back to be with the horses. Dani wished she could go, too, but that would be rude. "My name's Dani."

The man had on a frayed red jacket. He looked at her from her feet to the top of her head, what Dad called "sizing her up." "New around here, aren't you?"

Dani nodded.

The man pulled off his cap and slapped it against his leg. Dust billowed. "I'm Carl, the caretaker. Welcome to Racehorse Inn." He motioned her away with his hands. "Go on, look. I saw you staring at the horses. Just stay away from the temperamental sandy-colored one off by itself on the far end. He can be mean, tricky."

Dani raced to the nearest paddock. The horse seemed gigantic, lots bigger than she'd expected. Dani peered through the wooden rails. The back part of the pen had a little roof, probably to protect the horse from rain.

The animal was drinking from a trough. His ears flipped back against his head. Dani didn't think that was a good sign, so she went on to the next paddock. This horse was *bigger* and almost red. Dani sniffed. Everything smelled different here . . . furry, like mud, or the earth.

By the time she got to the third horse, a

brown one with big white patches, Carl limped up beside her. "You good with all animals? Or just dogs?"

Dani shrugged, pleased.

He held out a giant brush. "Anyone who visits, works," he announced.

"Brush the horse?" Dani looked straight at him. Even Carl's eyes reminded her of Dad's, the way they grinned when his mouth seemed serious. "Do you mean it?"

Carl patted the top of the fence. "Climb on up. Giana's a good paint. She'll stand for you." He whistled, and the brown and white spotted horse trotted over.

Dani couldn't believe her luck. She held her breath, then reached between the wooden slats with her finger and touched the rough fur. The horse felt magical. Dani imagined that riding her would be like running faster than the wind.

"Use this currycomb first," Carl explained.

Dani climbed to the top of the fence and held the round brush in both hands. She combed in a circle the way Carl showed her, to get out mud and stiff hairs. Giana snorted as if she were saying, "Ooh, that feels good!"

Then Dani switched to the flat body brush. She brushed and brushed until the horse's white patches shone.

Suddenly, she noticed the light fading. She had to get home and do her milking before dinner or Uncle Walter would be upset. Carefully, she set the body brush on the top rail of the fence. "'Bye, Carl!" Dani yelled.

"Mosey back sometime," he called.

She ran through the woods. At the stream she slipped on a rock. Dani raced into her yard and gave Tyler a big hug. "Did your shot hurt?"

She milked Jen, then hurried inside the house with the jar of fresh milk. Dani slid into her seat just as her uncle served dinner.

Uncle Walter scooped some mashed potatoes onto her plate. "Have a good afternoon?"

"Great!" Dani took a bite, though she knew she was supposed to wait for him to sit down. Mashed potatoes were her favorite. Dani noticed the dried green paint on the tip of her finger. Oops. She folded her green finger into her fist and held her fork with three fingers and a thumb. She wondered if Uncle Walter had gone down to his studio . . . if he had noticed the fingerprinted tree.

"Find any slimy snakes?" Clorissa asked.

Uncle Walter raised his eyebrows.

"I found a tigale!" Dani announced. She giggled. "The greatest discovery since . . . dinosaurs!" Right then and there, Dani decided that she'd keep the real discovery to herself. Racehorse Inn and her new friends would be her own special secret, at least for now.

5 Tyler's Trick

Dani tied her schoolbooks together with her belt and slung the leather strap over her shoulder like she'd seen in pictures in old storybooks. The books bumped against her back as she walked slowly home from the bus. Only two and a half more days until summer vacation.

A strangled cry in the distance jostled Dani out of her thoughts. She stopped and listened for a moment, but didn't hear anything else. Maybe she had imagined the sound.

Only two and a half days until she could spend all of her time with Tyler. Summer meant her tenth birthday, too, on July twenty-eighth, and time to visit Racehorse Inn. But Tyler would be most important. Since his birth six weeks ago, she had rushed home every day to practice for Plan T and to play with the little goat.

Dani kicked at the dirt and watched it fly. Every day but today. Today she didn't feel like rushing home.

A rich man from San Francisco was driving hundreds of miles to look at Uncle Walter's paintings this afternoon. He might hang some in his gallery, so people from all over the United States could buy them. Uncle Walter had told Dani and Clorissa that this could be the chance of a lifetime for him as a painter. He didn't want any wild people in the house, only perfect young ladies. Dani knew that he really meant her. Clorissa always acted like a perfect angel . . . around her dad.

The cry came again — a horrible scratchy wail. Could it be the goats? Dani swung her books into her arms and ran down the road. The awful sound grew louder. Dani threw open the outside gate and rushed into the yard. As she came into view of the house, she dropped her books and stumbled to a stop. The two baby goats stood on top of the porch roof, pressed tightly against each other, bleating at the top of their lungs.

That was impossible!

The porch roof was twice as far off the ground as the roof of the shed. Nothing, absolutely nothing, leaned against the porch roof for the goats to climb — no ramp, no plank. There was no way to get up there, even for the climbingest goat in the world!

Tyler saw her, and his voice grew shrill. I'm stuck up here, he baaed. He came right to the edge of the porch roof, put his hoofs in the rain gutter, and leaned forward into space.

"Don't you dare jump!" Dani yelled. She raced to the side of the house. As she'd hoped, both kids scampered away from the gutter to watch her. But then they kept running. Willy and Tyler clattered on up the two-story peak to the very top of the house. Now they were higher than the trees.

Dani stumbled into Jen's bony back. "Ooof!" She hadn't been watching where she was going. "Oh, Jen," she said. "At least you're on the ground." The mother goat pranced around her. Dani slowly circled the house. She couldn't find a single way to get up on that roof.

The farmhouse was built like the letter T, with an extra long top and a squat body. Dani had to jog around the little square jutting out of the back of the house. She couldn't even see a way onto the roof from the high landing at the top of the back steps.

Tyler had learned lots of tricks lately. He

41

could walk on his back legs. Three or four times a week now he hopped up on the kitchen windowsill and stared in while she and Uncle Walter and Clorissa ate their meals. Dani knew he was responsible for this stunt. Somehow.

As she rounded the front, Tyler slid down from the housetop and came trotting to the very edge of the porch roof again. He wobbled forward, farther and farther into space. "Tyler!" Dani rushed under him and held her arms up. She had to get him down before he fell!

Then she remembered that the man from San Francisco would be here soon. Dani gasped. Uncle Walter would be furious. She didn't want to be around, even if he was only mad at the goats.

If she could get the babies down before Uncle Walter got home, Tyler would be safe and her uncle grateful. She could tell him about how she had saved his day. Dani pounded one fist into her other palm as she decided what to do.

First, she pulled the small table off the front porch. Tyler peered over the rain gutter at her. His ears hung straight out like the blades of a toy helicopter. Next, she got the five-foot-tall aluminum ladder from the kitchen and a skein of Uncle Walter's light-weight rope that he used to hang pictures. He wouldn't mind. She unfolded the ladder and set it up on top of the table. Dani eyed the space between the top of the ladder and the gutter. She unwrapped the white rope in the dirt and took one end in her left hand.

Too bad Clorissa wasn't home from junior high yet. She was taller. Carefully, Dani crawled onto the table. As she climbed onto the first step, the ladder teetered. *Oooohhhh.* She climbed two more steps. Dani stuffed the rope into her teeth so she could grip the wobbly ladder with both hands. What if she fell? The ground looked a long way down.

The ladder leaned to one side and then the other. Dani's insides felt like the first time she had dived off the high board last summer. With a BUMP, the ladder finally stopped teetering.

Dani let go of the rounded top and straightened her body up into the air. She couldn't even breathe she was so scared. She reached out until her fingers clutched the rain gutter.

Now she had to catch the crying babies, tie the rope around their stomachs, and lower them to the ground. "Good babies," she tried to say, but the rope was still stuffed in her mouth.

Tyler stepped on one of her hands. Pain shot all the way down her arm. She didn't dare jerk away. The ladder might fall. As Dani's head came up over the edge, Willy nibbled on her hair. Dani swung one leg toward the roof, but her foot landed in the gutter instead.

Just then she heard a car pulling through the gate. What if it was the man from San Francisco? Here she was hanging from a rain gutter! The gutter creaked dangerously.

Uncle Walter's truck drove into the driveway. "Why was that gate left open?" he shouted. He leaped out of the truck. When he saw Dani, he looked astounded, then more furious than she'd ever seen him. Frantically, Dani tried to boost herself onto the roof.

Uncle Walter grabbed the ladder to steady it. His hand closed around her ankle. "Come down." His words sounded icy. "Can't you behave like a lady? Even for one day?"

"It's not my fault!" The rope fell out of

Dani's mouth and hit Uncle Walter on top of the head. "I had to get the goats down. For your meeting," she mumbled the last words.

"And kill yourself in the process?" Uncle Walter snapped. "What's wrong with you?"

Dani stumbled down the ladder, and Tyler and Willy began their ear-splitting cry again. When she was partway down, Uncle Walter put his arm around her waist and swung her roughly to the ground. Dani had the shivery feeling that he noticed her only when something went wrong. He yanked the ladder and the table away without saying a word. Dani felt her eyes start to fill with tears. She'd only been trying to help!

Uncle Walter started the truck with a roar and pulled forward under the porch roof. "Fool goats!" He swung himself into the open flatbed of the truck, but he still wasn't tall enough to reach them. Carefully, he crawled onto the cab roof, spreading his weight out so he wouldn't dent the top. "C'mon, Tyler. Willy."

They both backed away from him.

For a moment, Dani only watched. She folded her arms across her chest. She would back away from him, too.

Then Dani sighed. She knew how important this meeting was to her uncle . . . even if he was being unfair. She ran to the barn and came back with a big handful of hay dribbled with the molasses she'd bought with her allowance. Dani climbed into the back of the truck and hesitantly offered it to her uncle. He didn't even glare at her.

"Why today?" he muttered. He looked nervous, not so angry anymore. Willy came close enough to the hay for Uncle Walter to grab her by one leg. He pulled her along the porch roof toward him, and she began to bleat as if she were being killed. Jen jumped onto the open flatbed, baaing. Uncle Walter hooked his other hand under Willy's belly and swung the little goat down to Dani.

"Your turn, Tyler," Uncle Walter said in a false sweet voice. Tyler leaped forward and dipped his head, then bounded away. He stayed out of reach of Uncle Walter's long stretching fingers.

"I'm not playing!" Uncle Walter bellowed.

Dani heard another car in the driveway. "Uncle Walter!" she warned. She could tell by his expression that he had heard the car, too.

Uncle Walter lunged for Tyler and got him by one ear as the car pulled into the driveway. It was a big fancy white car. Tyler screeched. Uncle Walter's face turned bright red. He tucked Tyler under one arm and sat down on the top of his truck with a *thunk*. Tyler slithered free. Instead of jumping down into Dani's arms, Tyler slid down the windshield onto the hood of the truck. "My paint," Uncle Walter yelped.

Dani felt as if she were in the middle of a crazy movie.

The fancy car pulled up alongside the truck, and Tyler leaped onto its hood. The car screeched to a stop, then suddenly died. Inside, the man's mouth dropped open. Tyler knocked his bony forehead against the windshield with a loud clunk. His ears looked like helicopter propellers again.

"Aaahhh!" the man's voice shot way up high. "Remove that creature from my hood!" His face looked even brighter than Uncle Walter's.

Uncle Walter hopped out of the truck and went around to open the car door. He seemed to have recovered. "Just a goat. Nice to meet you. My name's Walter . . . Walter Benson."

The man flattened against the back of his

seat, staring. The knot of his tie bobbled up and down. Dani couldn't figure out why he was making such a fuss. Tyler hadn't made a dent in the car or scratched the paint. "Looks like a devil," the man whispered.

Dani started to giggle. She couldn't help yourself. Imagine! A grown man afraid of a baby goat. Uncle Walter glared at her. She clamped both hands over her mouth.

Uncle Walter scooped Tyler up in his left arm and held out his right hand to shake the man's hand. He motioned with his head for Dani. She rushed forward and took Tyler in her arms. Dani called to Jen, and Willy followed behind. She led all three goats back to the barn. She turned when she reached the shed. The skinny man was stepping out of his car, nervously straightening his coat. He tripped over the ladder in the dirt. Uncle Walter caught his elbow.

Dani sank to the ground. She didn't know whether to laugh at Tyler's car trick or cry. Uncle Walter had been awfully mad at her. Hanging from a gutter with a rope in her teeth — Dani could see now that even Mom would have been upset. "I sure haven't been a perfect little lady," she whispered to the goats.

"Lady!" a voice hissed behind her. "You wouldn't know how to be a lady if you had been raised by the Queen of England." Clorissa slipped out from behind the shed. "How could you have destroyed Dad's day, twerp? His special day?"

"You were hiding!" Dani declared as nastily as she could. Sometimes her cousin made her so mad!! Yet Dani found that she couldn't look at Clorissa.

Her uncle and the rich man disappeared inside. Dani squeezed Tyler and felt his bony back pushing into her stomach. *Had* she ruined Uncle Walter's day?

"I'm going to make them iced tea." Clorissa marched toward the house. "At least one of us can act like a human being."

Dani ripped up a solitary weed and threw it at Clorissa's back. She would never fit in with this family.

Tyler wriggled free and followed Clorissa. Halfway to the house, he reached out and took the back of her skirt in his mouth. Dani opened her mouth to warn her cousin.

Tyler swallowed, took a bigger bite, and threw his head sideways. Clorissa's skirt ripped all the way to her waist.

Dani yelped.

Clorissa screamed. She turned and swung an arm at Tyler. "You miserable little WRETCH!"

Dani leaped to her feet to protect her goat, but he'd already ducked away. Clorissa advanced another step.

Dani had to think of something, fast, or Clorissa would punish him. "Clorissa, your underwear!" she exclaimed.

Her cousin gasped. She twisted to look behind herself and flushed even more. Her pink underwear was showing. Desperately, Clorissa clutched her skirt closed with both hands. She trotted awkwardly into the house.

Dani couldn't help giggling. She lay back in the grass, remembering how Tyler had looked when he had leaped onto that car. That had been funny, too.

Tyler peered mischievously around the edge of the shed at her.

"Ah, Tyler." Dani's laughter stopped. "We got into a lot of trouble today." She rolled over and rested her chin on her arms. "I wonder what Uncle Walter is going to do to me."

The goat bleated as if he understood. He came close and butted her shoulder gently. Dani scratched the bony top of his head. "I wonder what Clorissa would like to do to *you*." Dani looked into Tyler's slightly crossed eyes. If only she could understand his goat speech. "Tyler? How did you and Willy *ever* get up on that roof?!"

6 Three Wishes

Dani turned an almost perfect cartwheel along the front porch. Her second hand came down inches from Uncle Walter's boot. He looked funny upside down, rocking in his chair.

A month of summer had passed, and no one had solved the mystery of the climbing goats. They didn't have a clue as to how Tyler and Willy had gotten on the roof. Dani still couldn't believe Uncle Walter hadn't punished her for climbing onto that rain gutter from a rickety ladder. The more she thought about it, the more she realized how dangerous that had been. Clorissa said she was lucky not to have been skinned alive . . . probably because the rich man from San Francisco had bought two paintings.

One other thing had changed since that day. Every time a car came down the dirt driveway, Tyler jumped onto the hood and stared in at the driver. Dani or Uncle Walter had to race outside and chase the little goat away.

With a pleased sigh, Dani plunked herself down onto the bottom step of the porch. It was nice to be all together. She and Uncle Walter hadn't fought in a week. Clorissa sat on the railing above, still in her nightgown, her hair perfectly combed. Uncle Walter had told Clorissa that she had to stay close to home this summer, so Dani wouldn't be alone as much. Clorissa had been spending every moment she could on the phone in the kitchen.

Jen and Willy ambled around the corner and nibbled on the grass. Now everyone was here, except Tyler. The little goat bounded around the shed, a bucket on his head. Dani giggled. He looked a little like those old-time carriage horses that wore giant flower hats that were too big for them.

Today Tyler had turned two and a half months old, old enough for the second step in Dani's plan to find him a home. She hadn't missed a day on his follow-the-leader lessons. He was well prepared for Plan T. Dani could hardly wait until they could be alone.

Tyler dropped the bucket off his head and kicked it with a clang.

"Score one for Tyler," Clorissa said.

The bucket flew underneath the porch. The goat peered wistfully into the dark space.

Dani got down on her hands and knees and crawled after the bucket. It was black as night under that porch. The envelope in her back pocket crinkled. Mom's latest letter was about castles and bell towers. Dani lay on her belly in the cool dirt. Lately Mom's letters sounded so happy that Dani sometimes wondered whether Mom might decide to stay in Oxford forever. The thought made her shiver in the darkness.

Since summer started, Dani didn't feel miserable during the days. She had Tyler for company. Besides, she'd visited the horse farm five times in the last month, each time while Tyler had been asleep and her uncle working. Clorissa never noticed. So, Racehorse Inn and Carl were still her secret.

After the sun set, though, Dani often sat alone in her attic cubbyhole. Then all of her fears crept back into her head: Uncle Walter didn't like her anymore. Clorissa considered her a pest. That's why her parents had left her — they didn't like her, either. Every night the thoughts swirled around in her head like little monsters.

Dani hooked the bucket with one finger and scooted back out from under the porch. Sunshine always banished the monsters. Tyler nibbled on her hair, and she pushed him gently away. He chewed on her finger instead.

"If you had three wishes, what would they be?" Uncle Walter asked absently.

Surprised, Dani climbed over the porch railing and dropped at his feet. This was the Uncle Walter she loved the most . . . the uncle who had always been her favorite. Ever since she had been a little girl, Uncle Walter had asked odd questions at family gatherings. He hadn't done that in months. Dani opened her mouth to answer.

"Mother alive again," Clorissa said in a tiny voice. She and Uncle Walter looked at each other in silence. Clorissa's Mom had gotten sick and died when Clorissa was only six. Dani's folks said that Uncle Walter had loved his wife like in a fairy tale.

Dani sat without moving, her mouth still open. She didn't have a mother for a year, but Clorissa didn't have one *forever*. Dani had never thought about it like that before . . . maybe because Clorissa never talked about her mother, or anyone's mother. Did Clorissa feel lonely at night, too? Or scared?

Suddenly, Dani felt like hugging her cousin.

With an abrupt switch of moods, Clorissa grinned. "Second wish. An old-fashioned blue velvet dancing dress without any shoulders that goes all the way to the floor." She twirled across the porch. "And a boyfriend!"

Dani groaned.

Uncle Walter laughed. He rocked a little faster. Then he leaned down and pinched Dani's toe playfully. "What about you?"

Dani was startled at his playfulness, but it felt good to be touched. She sat straighter. "First, I'd like to keep Tyler forever." She held up her second finger. "I want a rainbow that I could climb. A magic rainbow. I could slide down the other side of the rainbow and land anywhere I wanted. Like Oxford, to live with Mom!"

Uncle Walter was watching her. He was actually interested, *listening*.

Dani continued, grinning. "Third . . . I

want a new baseball suit, a uniform, so I could play with a real professional team. I'd be the only kid, the only girl." Dani stood up and swung an imaginary bat.

"How about a unicorn instead of a goat," Clorissa said softly.

"They're *my* wishes!" Dani exclaimed.

Clorissa ignored her. She looked at her Dad. "Then Dani would want a unicorn, a rainbow, and a baseball suit."

Dani turned to Uncle Walter for help. It wasn't fair for Clorissa to change her wish! But Uncle Walter's eyes had become unfocused again. He stood up so suddenly that the rocking chair tipped over behind him.

"A unicorn, a rainbow, and a baseball suit," he muttered. "That's good. I could paint that."

Clorissa smiled at his back as he left. Dani stared at him. He looked strange when he hung his head and moved his hands like that in midair. ". . . and a baseball uniform," he mumbled to himself as he disappeared inside.

He had left in the middle of a conversation, almost in the middle of a sentence. They had barely *started* to talk, the first good question Uncle Walter had asked in ages. Her uncle must be going to his studio. He hadn't invited her there once, since that day she'd rearranged his paints. He must have been very upset, because he'd even asked her not to go into his studio *at all.*

Clorissa closed her eyes and leaned back in the sun. "Have a rotten day," she said cheerfully. Clorissa always said nasty things in a nice voice. But she only did it when Uncle Walter was gone. Dani stood up. Her cousin had ruined the whole conversation. A few minutes ago she had wanted to hug Clorissa. Now she felt like pushing her off the railing.

7 Plan T, Step Two

Half an hour later, Dani sat by the gate scratching Tyler's bony back. Being alone with him always made her feel good. Besides, today was enormously important in Plan T.

It was time for step two.

They'd better get started before the day became too hot, and Tyler decided to take his afternoon nap with Willy and Jen. Dani thumped her goat gently. "Ready?"

Dani crawled back down the driveway a few feet to scout out the farm. Luckily, Clorissa still lay sunbathing with her eyes closed. Jen, with Willy by her side, munched on the bark of her favorite oak tree, so she wouldn't bleat and alert anyone. Uncle Walter, of course, was in his studio painting.

All clear to go ahead, Dani thought to herself.

She hurried back to the gate. Dani lifted the latch and pushed Tyler out of the yard.

She knew the goats were *never* allowed past the gate, but she had to take Tyler out if she were going to show him to all the neighbors and find him a home.

Carefully, Dani latched the gate behind them so the other two goats wouldn't follow. Then she climbed onto the stone wall that bordered the dusty road. Tyler hopped up behind her. She didn't need molasses-covered hay anymore. The little goat followed her as though she were his mother, his tiny tail straight up in the air, his white-tipped ears back. She was so proud of him.

Dani skipped along the top of the wall, and Tyler bounded along behind her, as if they were in a parade. Dani pretended she held a baton in her left hand and that she wore bright red boots. She could almost hear the parade music. Step, step. She lifted her knees high, then waved the baton. *The greatest goat in all the world,* she imagined the announcer saying. Dani turned to pat Tyler on the head.

He was gone.

"Tyler?!" She heard a crunch and ran back along the stone wall. She could see him, making a beeline for the neighbor's garden. All those leafy tops of carrots, even

the green tomatoes, must look *wonderful* to a goat.

Dani sprang over the dried up stream. One of her tennis shoes landed with a slurping sound in a deep patch of mud.

Now Tyler was chomping on a head of lettuce. Dani yanked her foot out of the sticky mud and hurried toward him. Tyler kept munching.

"Stop that!" Dani hissed and caught him by the neck. She expected the Wades to come out of the house and scream. Frantically, Dani herded Tyler back across the stream, waving her arms and hitting him on the rump. Perhaps Mrs. Wade would think that head of lettuce had been eaten by a giant snail. "This time you go in front," she announced.

But of course, Tyler wouldn't go first. Goats liked to follow. So Dani walked the stone wall with her head turned back. She couldn't lose sight of him for a moment. They took the shortcut through the woods.

Step two of Plan T called for taking Tyler to visit Carl and the horses. Dani knew that the horse farm wouldn't want a goat. Carl had said that the owner didn't want any more animals on the place . . . horses and a dog and some cats to catch the mice were enough. Today, Dani just needed to see how Tyler would behave on a visiting trip. She wanted Carl to meet him, too.

As she walked along the dirt path, Dani thought about her last visit to Racehorse Inn. Carl had let her exercise her favorite horse on the lunge line. Giana had run around and around that circular track while Dani held onto the rope. She'd written Mom that it had made her feel as though she were a champion, the way she'd felt the last day of school when her class baseball team had played the older kids and she'd been the winning pitcher.

Since exercising Giana, Dani had created another daydream for herself. She imagined herself working for Carl every day, maybe earning money. She could clean up at Racehorse Inn and brush the horses. Perhaps she'd even ride them.

Dani looked up to see Tyler prancing through the woods. He liked it out here. He dashed toward her, then jumped straight into the air as high as Dani's head. He landed hard on his front knees. Farther on, he leaped onto a branch of a tree to nibble on the leaves. Who ever heard of a goat climbing a tree? Dani thought. She laughed as he hopped to the ground with a leaf in his mouth.

Dani held up the barbed wire at the horse farm and scooted Tyler through. She had to shove on his bottom. Stubborn goat! Dani whistled for the guard dog, Nelly, to let her know that she was there. "Carl!" She waved to her friend. "Look who I brought to visit."

The big shepherd bounded toward them. Instantly, Tyler lowered his head. Nelly growled deep in her throat. She crouched so low that her belly nearly touched the ground. Her thick ruff stood straight up around her neck, and her lip lifted until all her teeth showed.

"Nelly?" Dani whispered. "Aren't you going to lick me?" The shepherd always kissed her. "It's *me*." Dani held out her hand for the dog to smell. Nelly ignored everything but the goat.

Carl ran toward them. "Don't you know that some dogs chase goats? Keep him calm!"

Dani had never seen Carl run before. He always walked slowly, with a bit of a limp. Dani turned her head to watch each step

Nelly took as she circled. "Stay close, Tyler." The dog's teeth looked sharper than Dani had ever noticed. Nelly looked like a cat stalking a mouse for dinner.

Carl lunged for the dog's collar and missed. He swore under his breath. Dani had never heard him swear, either. She could feel fear rising inside her like a wave.

The goat's eyes stretched wider, and he started to shake. His bleats got higher pitched. "Baaa. Baaa. Baa. Baa."

Silently and stiffly, Nelly crept toward the goat. Dani dove forward to tackle the shepherd's back legs. She didn't care if she did startle the dog into turning on her by mistake.

But Carl instantly caught Dani's overalls where they crossed in the back and pulled her upright. "I think it's all right now," he whispered. "Nelly doesn't look like she's going to pounce."

Inch by inch, Nelly smelled Tyler all over. Carl let out a deep sigh of relief as the goat relaxed. He patted Nelly's head. "Good girl. Never seen a goat before, have you?"

Dani leaned over and tried to gather Tyler into her arms. He was too big now. She glared at Nelly. Carl spoke fiercely above her. "Dani, you shouldn't take him around with you. Some dogs will chase goats until they drop dead. Or kill them by ripping out their throats!"

Dani's mouth already tasted as if she'd bitten into a rotten orange. Now her stomach sickened. What about Plan T? Dani's shoulders slumped, and she sat down in the dirt. What about showing Tyler to everyone?! If she couldn't take him out of the yard, then Plan T was *ruined.* The little goat squirmed free. Dani was so upset, she could hardly see.

Carl smiled. "Don't be so glum." He patted her on the shoulder. "Look, why don't you come brush Giana?"

Dani followed blindly. How would she ever find Tyler a home now?

"It must be pretty special to have a goat of your own as nice as that one," Carl said.

"What?" Then Dani realized what he had said. Neither Uncle Walter nor Clorissa noticed that Tyler was so nice. "He *is* special," she said. Tyler pranced along beside her. "He's smart, and he does tricks." Tyler must have been excited . . . he kept lifting his nose to smell the new scents. He sure had recovered fast.

She stopped at Giana's paddock and climbed up onto the fence. "Hey, girl," she said listlessly. Carl ambled back to finish cleaning out his tack box in the center of the clearing. Giana nuzzled at her pocket. Dani pulled out the carrot she had stuffed there earlier. The treat was covered with lint, but the horse didn't seem to mind. Her lips felt furry against Dani's open palm. In fact, they tickled.

Dani leaned forward and put her arms around the horse's neck. She wanted to race across field after field on Giana's back and forget everything. She only had six more weeks to find her little friend a home. Dani clutched the horse's mane. Plan T had failed. If only she could have those three wishes of Uncle Walter's *now* . . . or even only the first one. Dani closed her eyes and wished with all of her heart that she could live in a place where she could keep Tyler forever.

The railing shook a bit. Dani opened her eyes to see Carl climbing up beside her. "You always so impetuous?" he asked.

The word caught her attention. "What?"

"Jumping into things like an untamed colt," Carl explained. "That's impetuous."

Dani remembered hanging from the roof with a rope in her teeth. "My uncle would say I'm like that."

Carl wore his cap like Dad's. He had on the raggedy red jacket, too, that Dani liked so much. "Wild Colt," he said. "That'd be a good nickname for you."

Carl reached out toward the horse, whistling a song. Giana stepped forward and rested her head on his thigh. She snorted, in a loud sighing sort of way. Carl's song sounded sad, lonely. He broke off in the middle of the melody. "Better look out for that goat of yours."

Dani twisted around on the fence. Tyler couldn't stay out of trouble for an instant. "Where is he?"

"With Sands." Carl pointed down the row of horses.

"Sands?" Dani's chest tightened. She stayed away from that horse. Whenever anyone except Carl walked by Sands's paddock, he would rear up on his back legs, neighing loudly and kicking his front legs in the air. On one of Dani's first visits, before she understood his mean tricks, Sands had leaned way out of his paddock and nipped at her. He'd missed her arm, but he'd ripped one of her favorite shirts.

Sands had the last pen in the row. Dani stretched to see his paddock. Tyler stood right up against the gate. As usual, the big horse was running around and around the pen, snorting.

"Tyler," Dani called sweetly, but the goat didn't move. Dani slid off the fence and half ran and half tiptoed. She didn't want to startle either of them.

The next circle around, Sands stopped his racing with a sliding shower of dust. He peered down at Tyler, towering over the little goat. Then he snorted. Tyler still didn't move. Sands leaned his head out of the pen.

Dani danced in one place, clutching her hands together. Oh, please don't bite him, she pleaded silently. Please don't bite him. Carl's skinny body appeared at her side.

Tyler put his front paws on the outside of the gate and slowly stood up. Dani felt like screaming, but she was afraid to make a sound.

The horse and goat touched noses.

"Will you look at that?" Carl exclaimed. "That's my horse that doesn't get along with any of the other animals. But he's the best racehorse ever." Carl put his hand on her shoulder. "You sure have a fine goat, Wild Colt."

Dani knelt down in the dust, her knees too wobbly to stand. Tyler had eaten the neighbor's lettuce. Then Nelly had almost eaten him, and Plan T had been ruined. Now Tyler had made friends with Sands! "Yes, Tyler's all mine," she said shakily.

It was nice to talk as if Tyler were really hers . . . *forever.*

Dani sighed and looked up at Carl with his black cap. Perhaps she could pretend in this one place. She would pretend here with Carl that Tyler wasn't ever going to be sold for meat.

8 Spying on Tyler

July was too hot! At eight o'clock in the morning, Dani could already feel the sweat trickling down her back. If she and Clorissa didn't hurry, the goats would fall asleep in the heat and their spying trip wouldn't work. Dani hooked the gate shut and laughed as Tyler butted his head against the latch. When he stood on his back feet with his ears straight up, Tyler was almost as tall as she was now.

Dani hopped into the truck and slammed the door, gleefully. The truck shook, and Uncle Walter winced. She hadn't meant to close the door *that* hard. "We'll go with you as far as the Blakes' house, Uncle Walter."

"You two girls up to something?" Uncle Walter asked as they pulled onto the road.

Dani stared out the window. She didn't want to lie.

"We want to see their flowers," Clorissa answered. "I hear they have the prettiest flowers in the neighborhood."

Dani managed not to laugh. She kept her face sideways so Uncle Walter wouldn't see. Dani still couldn't believe that Clorissa had wanted to come today.

"Why don't you paint their flowers someday, Dad?" Clorissa continued.

Dani jiggled in her seat as they drove.

Clorissa had been nice lately. Maybe just because she was bored with summer. Dani hoped Clorissa had decided she liked her again. Last week she and Clorissa had sat together on her bed in the attic. Clorissa had offered to take a snapshot of Tyler with her camera so that Dani could carry the picture around to show people who might give him a home.

So Plan T was still alive! A photograph of Tyler might work. Dani crossed her fingers and toes whenever she thought about it.

Clorissa had secretly borrowed Uncle Walter's binoculars today. Both of them were sneaking up on the back of their own house to spy on Tyler. The little goats had somehow climbed onto the porch roof three times in the last week while Dani had been at the horse farm. She wanted to solve the mystery before Uncle Walter got too mad at Tyler or discovered her outings. Dani still hadn't told Uncle Walter about Racehorse Inn. She had this niggling little fear that he might not let her visit any longer.

Uncle Walter pulled to a stop before the Blakes' house, and Dani hopped out. Clorissa slid gracefully to the ground, one hand up to her mouth. "What lovely flowers!"

The flowers *were* pretty, like the postcard Mom had sent of an English garden. Dani turned back to the truck. "'Bye, Uncle Walter." She stepped toward the fence, then whispered to Clorissa. "Let's go." They had to cut through the Blakes' place to see their farmhouse from behind.

"Hold your horses." Clorissa grabbed onto the back of her shirt. Clorissa spoke out of the side of her mouth while waving to her father. "Wait until the big boss is out of sight."

Dani waved, too. When Uncle Walter was gone, she led the way under the fence. She held the bottom wire up for Clorissa. "The top row's barbed!" she whispered.

"I told you we had to be careful." Clorissa wiped the mud off her knees. She rolled her eyes. "Mrs. Blake hates children. She boils them in a pot in her backyard."

"Hah!" Dani looked at the windows of the white farmhouse. She crouched a little lower. The two girls crept through the rows of flowers in the side yard. Then Clorissa led them into a walled-in courtyard hidden in the back.

Dani instantly felt safer.

The walls of the courtyard stood taller than Uncle Walter. Luckily, two trees grew beside the wall nearest their own backyard. Dani swung herself up into the tree that looked the easiest to climb.

"The Blakes will see you up high," Clorissa whispered. "Can't you smell the smoke?" Her voice sounded spooky. "Mrs. Blake must be starting the fire to boil you in already. She only boils *little* children."

"I'm not little." Dani dropped from the branch of the tree onto the wall. She crouched as low as she could. This place was perfect! She could see their whole yard, yet she was far enough away so Tyler would never notice her. She motioned to Clorissa. "Come on!" Dani could see blobs moving along the side of the farmhouse. Three dark blobs. It must be Jen and the kids.

Clorissa stepped onto the wall. Her knee wobbled. She clutched at the branch as she sat down. Dani looked at her cousin in surprise — Clorissa was scared! Dani poked her. "Hurry up and get out the binoculars. I can see the goats."

All three blobs climbed up the back stairs to the door that led to Clorissa's bedroom. "Jen's checking the trash can," Clorissa muttered. She had the binoculars up to her eyes. "She's trying to knock off the lid. My empty potato chip bag is in there."

Clorissa's bedroom was on the second floor of the tiny square part of the house that jutted out in the back. The roof wasn't nearly as high as the main part of the house. On the left side, by the back landing, the roof almost fell away to the gutter it was so steep. On the other side, the roof sloped gently down. Clorissa loved the odd shape of her room.

"Let me see!" Dani whispered.

"In a minute, pest." Clorissa waved her hand away.

Dani glared at her. There wasn't anything else she could do, short of threatening to push Clorissa off the wall. The two little blobs dashed down the stairs and then back up.

Finally, Clorissa handed Dani the binoculars. She insisted on putting the strap around Dani's neck before she let her look.

Dani held the binoculars to her eyes. For a moment, she couldn't see anything but a blur. She moved the little wheel above her nose and found the goats so suddenly that she jerked backward. It was as if they were a few feet away. Dani could feel Clorissa's hand between her shoulder blades. There was Tyler! She could even see his mischievous expression.

Tyler stood on the back porch. With a tiny hop, he bounded up onto the railing. Then he stepped out with one foot onto the rain gutter. Dani gasped.

"Is that pint-sized rascal doing what I think he's doing?" Clorissa exclaimed, tugging on the binoculars.

Dani gripped the binoculars so hard that her hands hurt, and she leaned away from Clorissa. The narrow gutter was a whole story above the ground. If Tyler fell, he would be killed.

Tyler pranced forward. He had all four feet in the rain gutter now! He ran along the gutter until he reached the sloping roof of the main part of the house. Then he zipped to the peak. Dani could barely hear his tiny bleat. For some reason, Willy didn't follow.

"*Brainless* pint-sized rascal!" Clorissa

cried. "That rain gutter isn't supposed to hold any weight."

Tyler looked so proud. He trotted back and forth along the top of the roof. Dani couldn't resist laughing. "Do you suppose circuses ever take goats?"

Tyler disappeared down the other side of the roof. Dani knew he was sliding to the porch roof. In a moment, he reappeared and pranced along the top again.

Clorissa grabbed Dani's arm and yanked so hard that the binoculars jerked down from her face. "It's still my turn!" Dani cried.

Clorissa clamped a hand over her mouth. "Look!"

A plump woman in a faded dress was walking up one row of the flower garden they had sneaked through earlier. She carried a handful of flowers and clippers. She had a cane hooked over her arm.

Dani dropped the binoculars onto her chest and jumped for a limb of the tree. In another second, Mrs. Blake would catch them. Dani swung herself to the ground. Clorissa stood up on the wall very slowly. She was as visible as a spotted brown giraffe against a blue sky.

"Hurry!" Dani exclaimed softly. Clorissa

couldn't get turned around right. What was wrong with her? Dani scrambled up into the tree and helped guide her cousin's foot to a branch. She wasn't even wearing tennis shoes. How could you climb a tree in loafers?

"I can't do it!" Clorissa whispered. "I can't." She sounded terrified. "I haven't climbed down a tree in years! I never liked climbing down trees."

Clorissa needed her help! Dani guided her cousin's feet down one by one. "Of course you can do it."

"Darn tree. Darn shoes," Clorissa muttered. Her face looked pale. "This is all your fault. He's your goat."

Then Dani smelled something. Smoke! Dani yanked her cousin down the last jump. Clorissa fell on top of her, but neither of them made a sound.

Dani scrambled out from under Clorissa and rushed for the gate of the little walled courtyard. The woman couldn't really boil children. She couldn't!

Still . . . she might be crazy. Dani's heart pounded. The only way out of the courtyard was past that woman. Dani crept closer to the gate, then froze as she noticed Mrs. Blake looking straight at her!

9 Boiling Barrel and Barbed Wire

Dani flattened herself against the wall of the little courtyard. Clorissa joined her, and their shoulders touched. Dani just knew that she and Clorissa would be caught . . . any second now.

Mrs. Blake came to the end of the flower row. She clipped an orange rose, then turned and started up the next row, her back to the two girls. She must not have seen them!

Dani peered out the gate.

"You got me into all this," Clorissa hissed behind her.

To her left, Dani could see the smoke now. Smoke drifted out of the big barrel set in a small cleared area. Mrs. Blake walked farther and farther away.

Clorissa shoved Dani's shoulder. The two girls slipped out of the gate together and ran toward the back of the house, right past the flames. Dani tried to see what was in the barrel, but she couldn't stretch tall enough.

Dani glanced over her shoulder and gasped as she saw Mrs. Blake. The woman had started down the next row. She was standing still, examining a yellow flower. So she was facing them again. If she looked up . . .

Both girls fell onto their stomachs behind tiny bushes. The dirt was damp. Yet they stayed motionless. Mrs. Blake worked her way down the row. Every time she turned her head their way, Dani stopped breathing.

Instead of going up the last row, the woman walked toward the fire . . . toward them! Dani ducked her head. She couldn't hear Clorissa's breathing anymore, only those soft footsteps and the bubbling crackling sound of the fire.

What would Mrs. Blake do to them? What kind of a person would put barbed wire on her fence? Dani knew she would turn blue if she didn't breathe soon. She heard Mrs. Blake stir whatever was in that barrel with her cane. Then the footsteps moved away.

Soundlessly, Dani raised herself to her feet and zipped, all bent over, through the backyard to the opposite side of the house. Then she ran up the side yard. Behind her, Clorissa sounded like an elephant crashing through the underbrush. But no one tried to stop them. Dani dove and rolled under the fence. She held up the bottom wire for Clorissa. "That was close," she panted. They were safe now, back on the street. Dani grinned.

Her cousin turned on her so furiously that Dani backed away a step. "If anyone ever finds out about this," Clorissa cried, "I'll be laughed at by the whole high school. High school!" Her mouth twisted. "Tell anyone, you hear, and I'll . . . I'll . . ." Clorissa spluttered. "I'll tear up your picture of Tyler." She tried to wipe the mud off her cheek but only smeared it. "Look at me! I've never been so embarrassed in my whole life! Crawling through the mud!"

"I won't tell, Clorissa. I . . . I won't tell *anyone*," Dani said. She couldn't resist grinning again. "But you have to admit it was exciting."

Clorissa looked as if she were going to strangle her.

Dani felt like a can of soda that had been shaken and then opened. She couldn't stop bubbling. "Even climbing down that tree was fun." She danced around and chuckled. "And *you* were scared. I've never seen you really scared."

Clorissa reached out and grabbed her shoulder, hard.

Dani gasped at the look in her cousin's eyes. Her feet froze to one spot, and she couldn't even seem to open her mouth to apologize.

"Another thing, creep," Clorissa said. "I never asked you to come live with us."

The last of Dani's excitement seeped out of her like air from a pricked balloon.

"I never wanted you here," Clorissa hissed. "I never wanted you at all."

Dani reached for her cousin with one hand. "NO!" The sound didn't come from her lungs. It came from her heart and deep down in her guts.

Clorissa slapped her hand away.

Horrified, Dani stared at her hand for a moment. Then she twisted around so fast that she slipped in the grass. She ran down the road. That's why Clorissa hadn't liked her this year. She hadn't wanted Dani to live with them in the first place! Uncle Walter probably didn't want her, either.

All her terrible feelings had been true. She was just in the way!

Dani ran toward home until she couldn't tell whether she was panting or sobbing. She would run away! That's what she would do. Uncle Walter and Clorissa didn't want her. Neither did her parents. Nobody wanted her!

Dani ran and ran and ran, all the way to Uncle Walter's. She stumbled into the yard. Tyler began crying piteously from the porch roof. Dani stared up at him. Her lungs hurt. She couldn't run away, not with Tyler here. She had to find him a home.

Dani headed for the shed. She'd show Uncle Walter and Clorissa. She'd wait until she found Tyler a home, then she'd run away. Tyler's cries hurt her ears. He sounded the way she felt inside. "I won't leave you up there, Tyler," she cried over her shoulder. "Not the way Mom and Dad left me." Dani's tears made it hard to see to scoop oats into the bucket and dribble molasses over them. She walked to the back steps. "Tyler!"

The little goat appeared on the very top of the house.

Clorissa came into the yard. She was panting. "See if I ever believe you again, crazy goat," she yelled at Tyler. "You aren't stuck. You can get down anytime you want."

"He's not crazy!" Dani snapped as she climbed the stairs.

Clorissa looked up at her and then at the gutter. "I hope that rain gutter holds one more time. I'll stand underneath to catch Tyler if he slips."

"Just go away," Dani whispered fiercely. She didn't care if Clorissa heard her. Dani never wanted to see her cousin again. She put one foot up on the railing and waved the bucket of oats. "Tyler!" What if the gutter did break? Tyler bleated and raced down the slanted roof. Dani held her breath as he pranced along the rain gutter toward her. How could he balance on that tiny strip of metal? She heard Clorissa gasp.

But Tyler made it across. He balanced half on the railing and half on the gutter as he stuck his nose into the bucket. Dani kissed him on the top of the head and yanked him down with every bit of her strength onto the landing. Then she used the bucket to entice him all the way down the steps and around to the front porch. She plunked herself down on the bottom stair, feeling as if her body were made out of wet quivering noodles.

Clorissa dropped beside her with a sigh. "That was close. Dad will have to nail a piece of wood up between the railing and that gutter tonight."

Dani slid as far away from Clorissa as she could. Her cousin was acting as if *nothing* had happened. Dani sat scrunched up against the post, holding the bucket so that Willy and Jen could get part of the treat. Clorissa was acting as if they were friends the way it had seemed earlier today and last week. Why didn't she go away?

"That was pretty close, wasn't it?" Clorissa repeated. After a second, she said, "Mrs. Blake would be horrible to have for a mother, wouldn't she?"

This time Dani looked at her. Clorissa almost never said the word *mother*. Her cousin sat straightening her shoe, her eyes on the ground.

"That old lady almost boiled you," Clorissa teased. Her arm darted out, and she lightly ruffled Dani's hair. Still, she didn't look at her.

Dani spoke before she could stop herself. "Did you mean what you said today?" Her voice broke. "About not wanting me to live here?"

Clorissa looked at her now, right at her. "Dani, I was furious about being dirty. Then you *laughed* at me." Clorissa clenched her fists and screamed, "I was really MAD!

Besides, it's been a *drag* this summer having to stay home so much."

Dani jumped up to get away. Tyler and Willy bleated because she pulled away the last nibble of their treat.

In one of her quick changes of moods, Clorissa sighed and half smiled. "Other than that . . . of course, I want you here. Who could resist having a little sister to pick on for a year?"

Dani dropped the bucket with a clatter and stared. Clorissa looked like she meant it. Dani's eyes tingled. She'd wanted a sister for as long as she could remember. Being a sister was better than being a cousin . . . or even a friend. Wasn't it? Dani felt the hurt inside beginning to melt. Clorissa was mad about losing her freedom, but she still liked her. Dani could understand that.

Tyler ate the last bite of the oats, then chewed on the metal bucket. Willy zipped in and kicked the bucket with a clang. The two young goats raced off side by side.

Dani reached to touch her cousin's shoulder. This time Clorissa didn't slap her hand away. Dani grinned shyly.

Sisters always fought now and then . . . right?!

10 Rocking Goat

Dani ducked underneath the wire fence into the horse farm. Nelly bounded up to her and kissed her from her chin to her nose. Dani spluttered. The dog kissed her again. "How did you know it was a special day?" Dani scratched Nelly behind the ears and added in a whisper, "Today would be perfect if Mom weren't in England."

"Mule Day?" Carl called. "Is that why it's so special?" He stood in the middle of the yard checking Giana's feet. The horse had been saddled up.

"Nope." Dani skipped toward him. She liked saying "Nope" the way he did. Dani hopped as high as she could on each foot. She could hardly keep from blurting out the truth.

"Let's see now. . . . Compliment Your Mirror Day?" Carl solemnly flicked a pebble out of Giana's hoof with the hoof pick.

"No, sir!" Dani stopped skipping. "You made that one up."

Carl crossed his heart. "You haven't heard of Compliment Your Mirror Day?! National holiday, girl. You're supposed to compliment your mirror on having such a wonderful owner."

Dani laughed.

"July twenty-eighth . . . NOW I remember!" Carl snapped his fingers as Dani came close. "July twenty-eighth must be the annual Chicken Clucking Contest. I went one year. Amateur chicken cluckers from all over the country met in Baltimore. They competed for trophies of giant chickens."

Dani turned a cartwheel. "It's my birthday!!" she cried, upside down.

"Aaaaaahhhhh," Carl answered.

Dani came out on her feet and noticed two other people in the horse paddocks, grooming and saddling up horses. The County Fair would begin in two and a half weeks. Racehorse Inn was full of excitement these days. Giana would run her first race at the Fair. She was two years old. The chestnut named Chessy would be jumping. Old spotted Elmer had been entered in an event that involved a lot of fancy footwork. Dani could never remember the name. It sounded something like dressing.

Carl checked Giana's last foot. "So . . . you thirteen years old today?"

Dani wiped the sweat off her forehead. She giggled and shook her head.

"Now, you're not fifteen!" Carl pretended to be amazed. "Aren't you kind of little?" Carl patted Giana. "Ever thought of taking up chicken clucking? You'd probably be a natural, seeing as how the contest is on your birthday and all."

Dani rested her face against Giana's nose. The horse nickered affectionately.

Carl held onto the reins and pointed to Giana with his other arm. "Climb on up, Birthday Girl."

The moment stopped for Dani. Even the wind didn't blow for an instant. Climb up? He was going to let her ride?

The edges of Carl's mouth curled up into a big smile. This must be his birthday present to her! He cupped his right hand. "Need a boost?"

She put her foot into his hand, and he lifted her into the air. Dani grasped wildly for the saddle and landed on her stomach across Giana. The horse danced sideways.

"Easy, girl," Carl whispered, almost singing.

Awkwardly, Dani threw her leg over the

wide brown back and sat up, clutching the saddle horn.

She looked *down* on Carl's head. She was so high that she could see over the trees and out of the yard. Wait until Mom heard about this! Maybe they would be able to ride together when Mom got back.

Giana felt warm against Dani's legs. "It's me. Your friend." Then Dani clicked at her the way she'd heard Carl do. To her surprise, Giana stepped forward. She lifted her head so proudly.

"Hold on," Carl said. He adjusted her stirrups. Then he walked the horse around the yard, telling Dani how to keep her heels down and how to use the reins to steer. "Only one rule. No running. You encourage Giana to run, you get down." He handed her the reins. "Go anywhere in the yard, except near Sands."

Dani couldn't believe her luck. "Thanks!" Then she hummed, "Happy birthday to me."

Giana headed straight for the tack box, where Carl stored the treats. Dani yanked on the reins. The horse kept going for the goodies.

"Hold them low," Carl called.

Hold what low? Dani wondered. Then

she noticed that she was holding the reins up around her chest. Ooops. She lowered them to the saddle horn and pulled to the left, gently this time. Giana snorted at her, but she turned away. "It worked!" Dani cried. "Good girl!" She reached down to pat Giana and nearly slipped off, headfirst.

Dani walked the horse around the paddocks. Giana wanted to visit with all the horses, so it was hard. Carl sat in the middle of the yard repairing tack. When Dani came by, he said, "I want Giana to look real pretty for the race, Wild Colt. And she sure likes you. If you're at the fair Saturday, how about stopping by to help groom her?"

"I'd love to!" Dani cried.

The magical feeling of sitting on top of Giana stayed with Dani all afternoon. After an hour of riding, she brushed Giana until her white patches shone. Then Dani headed home to play with Tyler. As usual, she won at tag, but Willy and Tyler beat her in the racing games.

After a race from the front porch to the shed, Tyler stood on his back legs to show off. Dani danced with him. He was *so* good at tricks. She wished the neighbors she'd shown Tyler's picture to this past week had wanted him. If only they could see him playful like this. Dani bowed at the end of the dance, and Tyler dropped to all four feet, ducking his head, too.

Clorissa threw open the front door with a crash. She tore out into the yard. "The phone's for you!" Dani had never seen her cousin so excited. She hurried inside and picked up the phone.

"Hey, pumpkin," a familiar voice cried. "I'm calling from New York. I got in from France last night."

"Dad!" Dani screeched. His voice sounded warm and deep, like a hug. He told her he had sent a French toy . . . a bird that could fly all by itself. They talked for fifteen glorious minutes.

As Dani hung up, Uncle Walter arrived home in the truck. He had a present from Mom. Dani could tell the package was a book. "I'll open it with the others." She hugged the book in her lap until they sat down to eat dinner. Uncle Walter had let her pick her favorite foods, so she'd chosen all the bacon she could eat.

"Yuck!" Clorissa exclaimed. "Bacon with mashed potatoes?" She picked up her napkin to dab at the corner of her mouth. Then she stuck her tongue out at Dani.

Dani nibbled on nine pieces of bacon and three servings of mashed potatoes. Finally, Uncle Walter made her close her eyes. Dani could hear scurrying footsteps and packages being set on the table. When Clorissa and Uncle Walter started singing, Dani opened her eyes to see a giant chocolate cake. "How did you know chocolate was my favorite?"

"Secret sources." Uncle Walter set a red crown on her head at the end of the song. "Ta Da! The Birthday Queen!"

Dani laughed. She couldn't believe how playful he was being. Dani reached for the present from Mom and ripped apart the paper. It was a big book titled *Stories about English Castles*. On the inside cover, Mom had written:

TO DANI . . . a scary book to read all by yourself with a flashlight.
Happy Birthday, Darling! May this special day bring you lots of joy, and may this year bring us back together again *soon*. Love, love, LOVE,

Mom

The next present turned out to be a necklace of shiny orange beads from Clorissa. Dani didn't wear necklaces, but she liked the color. "Thanks."

Clorissa grinned back. "Let me put it on you. The orange stones will look great with your purple T-shirt."

They all heard a *clunk* against the window. Dani knew what that sound meant before she even looked. Tyler! The goat was standing on the window ledge cheerfully staring in at them.

"He must have heard the singing," Uncle Walter said. "Mighty unusual goat. I've been raising goats for twenty years, and I've never had one like him."

Tyler bleated.

"Can we let him in?" Dani begged. "Please, Uncle Walter? Just this once?"

"A goat inside the house?" Clorissa rolled her eyes.

"No," Uncle Walter said firmly. Then he added, "If you want him to join your party, we can go outside." Dani grabbed the remaining present, a flat package from Uncle Walter, and led the way outdoors. Clorissa brought the cake, and Uncle Walter carried the plates. They put the cake and utensils on the tiny table by the rocking chair.

Tyler walked all around Dani on his back legs. He nibbled on her shirt. Dani balanced the shiny red birthday crown on his head. "I want to be a veterinarian when I grow up." She glanced shyly at her uncle.

"Animals sure like you," Uncle Walter said. "But we don't need a goat-nibbled crown around here." He took the crown away from Tyler and put it back on Dani's head.

Dani wished she and Uncle Walter could always get along this well. Willy and Jen stood in the yard. Uncle Walter sat in his rocking chair, and Dani and Clorissa sat on the railing. "My last present," Dani said. She felt like ripping the package open, but for some reason she opened the paper very carefully. She was glad she had. Inside was a drawing . . . a drawing of a horse!

"Drew that last January," Uncle Walter said. "Just about the time you arrived."

Dani looked at the horse carefully, at the white patch on the brown head, at the expression. "It's Giana!" she cried. "Oh, thank you, Uncle Walter. What a perfect gift."

Her uncle looked surprised. "How do you know her name?"

Dani gasped. She put her hand over her

mouth. The skin all over her body prickled as she realized what she'd said.

"Dani," her uncle insisted.

First, Dani shakily set the picture down on the railing beside her. Then she told her uncle all about her secret visits to Racehorse Inn. She left out the part about taking Tyler. Dani's voice got quieter and quieter. "Carl let me ride Giana today. He wants me to help groom her for the fair," she finished.

No one spoke. Even Tyler remained silent. All Dani could hear was the creaking of her uncle's rocking chair.

"But I don't understand," Uncle Walter finally said. He sounded puzzled. "Why didn't you tell me?" When Dani didn't answer, his expression changed. His eyes narrowed, and he bit down on his lower lip. Then he got up from his chair in a rush.

"Dad, don't be mad," Clorissa whispered. "It's her birthday."

Uncle Walter paced along the porch. Dani felt her heart tumbling toward her shoes. The picture of Giana was so good! She *knew* she should have told him where she'd been going. That was one of Mom's biggest rules. "I'm sorry," she pleaded. But Uncle

Walter didn't have the right to get angry at her on her birthday, did he?

At that very moment, Tyler leaped into the moving rocking chair and slid to the back. He twisted himself around and sat upright in the chair. Tyler threw his head forward. Then, at the proper instant, he leaned back.

"That little twerp is rocking on purpose!" Clorissa cried. "Unusual isn't the word for him. Goats can't rock in chairs!"

Tyler rocked back and forth again. He eyed the chocolate cake.

"What a trick!" Dani exclaimed. "A new one!" She stood up on the railing and clapped her hands above her head. "Tyler's birthday present to *me.*" The goat kept rocking.

Clorissa giggled. Even Uncle Walter began to chuckle.

They voted unanimously to give Tyler a piece of the cake.

11 Lettuce and the Bedspread

In the eleven days since her birthday, Dani had spent most of her time visiting neighbors to show them Tyler's picture. Today, it had taken her over an hour to walk home. She was nearly there. Dani kicked furiously at the dust in the dry stream bed. No one wanted Tyler. No one! She could only think of two or three more homes that she could visit.

The entire summer she'd been secretly hoping for a miracle. She'd been dreaming that Uncle Walter would change his mind and let her keep Tyler. Or she'd hoped that a circus owner would drive into the driveway, and Tyler would leap onto the hood of the car. Then the circus owner would fall in love with the goat and take him away to be famous forever.

Dani threw a pebble at a tree in front of her. Now summer was almost over, and Tyler was three and a half months old *today*. Lately, Dani's mind had been filled with a hideous vision. She kept imagining a family of four sitting at a table to eat dinner. They all held knives. The father was cutting into a chunk of meat that looked like Tyler's curious face.

Dani swallowed against the panic growing inside of her. She only had two more weeks to find him a home.

Mother hadn't written since her birthday, either, not even a postcard. It had never been this long before. Dani folded her arms across her chest. She wanted to sit down in the dirt and howl as if she were only five years old.

Slowly, Dani rounded the last corner in the road before the driveway. The scrunching of a footstep made her look up.

Uncle Walter stood on the stone wall beside their gate. He didn't see her. This week he'd stayed home, taking time off his job to paint. Clorissa had declared herself free. She'd been riding her bike all over the countryside to visit friends.

"JEN!!!" Uncle Walter bellowed.

Dani clamped both hands over her ears, the yell was so loud. What was wrong? Then she saw that the gate to their yard stood wide open.

Uncle Walter jumped off the wall and

ran across the stream bed into the tall grass. The goats must be out!

Dani raced after her uncle, then skidded to a stop, horrified. Willy and Jen stood right in the middle of the Wades' garden! Jen looked up happily at Uncle Walter with a giant bean plant hanging from her mouth. The garden didn't look like a garden at all. Most of the carrot tops had been chewed to the ground. The corn had been trampled.

Willy chomped through the stem of a zucchini plant.

A short distance away, Tyler stood under the clothesline. He liked cloth. Dani could see holes in the bedspread that hung beside him.

"Fool goats!" Uncle Walter's voice cracked. He waved his arms, but none of the goats moved. Uncle Walter whomped Jen on the back end with the flat of his hand. Dani could hear the slap. She'd never seen Uncle Walter hit anything! With a startled *baaaa*, Jen bounded out of the garden. Willy followed.

Tyler took another bite of the bedspread. Uncle Walter stepped toward him so menacingly that Dani rushed between her uncle and the goat. Every muscle in her body trembled. Dani stood with her back to Tyler, her arms out to protect him. Her tongue stuck to the roof of her mouth so she couldn't make a sound.

Tyler chose that moment to stick his head out between her legs.

"Your goat!" Uncle Walter pointed at her and took one step closer. Tyler's head popped back. Uncle Walter's face was bright red. "He opened that gate!"

Dani stepped away. "It wasn't just Tyler!"

Uncle Walter dropped both hands to his sides and clenched them into fists. He stared down at Dani. Dani stared back at him defiantly, then dropped her eyes. She *had* seen Tyler playing with the latch on the gate. She remembered him butting at it that morning she'd gone spying with Clorissa. Willy and Jen never played with that latch, only Tyler. Dani could feel Tyler nibbling on the back of her shirt.

"Look at this garden," Uncle Walter hissed. "Ruined. And that bedspread. We're going to owe these people money. Money that I don't have right now. Money that I will have to earn. And earning money takes me away from my painting!" Uncle Walter tapped his chest with his finger. "I've been nice, because you love that goat. Now it's time to be getting rid of him."

Dani felt as if her heart missed a beat, then missed again. "I've got two more weeks!" Her voice came out barely a whisper.

"Not if he's going to teach the other goats bad tricks. What will I do if Jen learns to open that gate?" Uncle Walter stood straighter. He looked as tall as a giant again. Uncle Walter pointed his whole arm at Tyler. "I just may sell that goat tomorrow."

12 Tyler's Last Chance

Three hours later, Dani hesitated at the doorway of the kitchen. Then she stepped forward to face Uncle Walter. She had dirt caked under her fingernails from working in the neighbor's garden. All afternoon . . . every minute . . . she'd felt as if someone were setting off giant firecrackers inside her head.

"Sit down, Dani," her uncle said.

But Dani refused. She had to know if Uncle Walter really meant to sell Tyler tomorrow. Dani hung onto the kitchen table with both hands. Her uncle fiddled with the ring on his finger. His hands were dirty, too. Dani imagined him throwing Tyler into the back of his truck.

Her uncle looked anywhere but at her. "I know you tried to find Tyler a home. You tried hard."

This was worse than any nightmare Dani had ever known . . . Uncle Walter was being nice about destroying Tyler. She had to speak to her uncle and convince him to give her more time. The goat was her *best* friend. But Dani couldn't find a single word to say.

"Dad!" Clorissa burst into the room and stood by Dani's side. She laid one hand next to Dani's. In her other hand dangled a short thick chain and a clip.

Dani gripped Clorissa's fingers so hard she was afraid she would hurt them. Her cousin knew how to talk to Uncle Walter, didn't she? Clorissa spoke sweetly, even smiled a bit. "We could clip the gate shut with this extra chain. Then the little latch-pushing twerp couldn't get free."

Dani sucked in her breath.

"Well, now . . ." Uncle Walter looked up at Dani, and she begged him with her eyes. Uncle Walter stood up so fast that his chair fell over. "You're just putting it off, girl. You're making it harder on yourself."

"Please," Dani whispered.

Uncle Walter threw his hands into the air, and let them fall. Then he turned. "Two more weeks," he said as he strode out of the room.

When the door closed behind him, Clorissa cheered softly. "Hurray!" Dani leaped on top of the table.

"Stop that!" Clorissa exclaimed. "You'll be fried alive if he comes back."

Dani danced on the table. Tyler was hers again! She had two more weeks to find him a home. Somehow she would succeed. She knew she would! Maybe a miracle *would* happen.

Dani stopped dancing and bowed with a wide flourish to Clorissa. She meant to say something royal, but all that came out was, "Clorissa, you're the best big sister in the whole world."

The days of the next week, the last days of summer, passed one by one until Tyler only had seven days left before he turned four months old. Dani leaned against the fence to read the letter that had come from Mom. This past week she had thought about her mother more than she had for ages. Dani knew that if she found Tyler a home, she'd be lonely. If she didn't find Tyler a home, it would be more terrible than she could even imagine.

Dear Listy Dani,
  I loved your last letter. Your list of birds that you have seen was wonderful. Did you really see a condor?!

I enjoyed knowing the books you've read this summer, too. Have you discovered *The Borrowers* yet? It's a story about a girl who finds a family of little people who live in the walls of her hearth. They become her best friends. It's a series, so if you like one, you'll have a lot of books to read.

I'm off to have a real English tea with a friend. We'll have scones and jam and thick, thick cream.

I love you! Give my love to Walter and Clorissa. I'll write soon this time, I promise.

Hugs!
Mom

P.S. Scones are fancy biscuits. Yum!
P.P.S. Pat a horse for me.

Carefully, Dani folded the letter and put it back in her pocket. She'd think about finding that book next week when school started . . . when she didn't have Tyler. Dani took a deep breath.

Today was the County Fair. That meant this afternoon she would help groom Giana for her race. Dani had also come up with one final idea to use the fair to find Tyler a home.

She had visited every neighbor now. Each afternoon after working in the garden, she'd taken the bus to another area. No one wanted Tyler.

Plan T had failed. Miserably.

Dani knew this was Tyler's last chance. She laid the two sides of her giant cardboard box and her black marking pen out on the front porch. As she worked, Tyler jumped up onto the railing from the ground and peered down at her. He was so curious. His ears still looked like a helicopter's propellers when he leaned over. A lot of the time Dani spent with him she felt sad inside. She wrote the same words on each sign in big letters. MALE TOGGENBURG GOAT FOR SALE, Four Months Old. What else should she write? People would want to know what he was like. So she wrote CHEERFUL ACROBAT.

Tyler jumped down and landed with his front feet together right on one of her signs. "Tyler!" He pushed against her with his head and almost knocked her over. Dani grabbed his leg and quickly outlined one of his feet with the marker. Then she labeled it TYLER'S PRINT.

Next she poked holes in the top of each

sign and tied the two signs together with heavy string. She slipped them over her head and marched around the porch. The sign on her front thumped against her knees with every step. Tyler pranced along behind her.

An hour later, Uncle Walter drove Dani and Clorissa to the fair. Dani sat in the window seat, as far away from her uncle as possible. She had barely talked to him all week. She couldn't forget what he had looked like in the garden, standing over her with his fists clenched.

Uncle Walter stopped a block early in the heavy traffic. Dani jumped down and slipped her signs over her shoulders. "'Bye. See you at dinner."

"Dani," Uncle Walter called. "Come here."

Hesitantly, she went around to his window. She stood far enough away so the signs wouldn't hit the truck. Uncle Walter dropped a package wrapped in green tissue paper into her hands. "I couldn't manage a whole uniform," he said. "And I know you like green." Then he pulled away.

"But — " Dani watched in amazement as the truck disappeared. Why had Uncle Wal-

ter given her a present when it wasn't even her birthday?

Clorissa grinned at her. "See, he's not such an ogre." That made Dani feel embarrassed. Uncle Walter *was* Clorissa's father. Her cousin pushed her on the back to get her out of the center of the street. "He's the silent type. So you have to talk to him. Laugh with him."

Dani looked at the package in her hands, then at her cousin. Laugh with that big giant man? He hardly did anything but daydream, and he almost never smiled. But he had given her this present. Dani ripped open the green tissue paper. Inside lay a new green baseball cap with "A's" printed across the front. It had a bright yellow brim. "A real cap!" Dani cried. Uncle Walter had given her a new baseball cap, a professional one like the players wore.

"A unicorn, a rainbow, and a baseball suit," Clorissa whispered.

"A goat, not a unicorn," Dani corrected. "A goat, a rainbow, and a baseball suit." Uncle Walter had said he couldn't manage a whole uniform . . . so he'd given her a cap. Now she could pretend she was a player with the Oakland A's. She'd be the only kid and the only girl.

Then Dani stumbled in the middle of a perfectly flat sidewalk. Her uncle had tried to give her one of her three wishes! Did that mean he wanted her wishes to come true?

Dani cradled the hat against her chest. Her eyes stung. Perhaps Uncle Walter did try to understand her . . . even if he never read to her or hugged her. Gently, Dani ran her fingers over the bright yellow brim.

"Hey, Zombie." Clorissa yanked the new baseball cap out of her hands and pulled it down over Dani's eyes so she couldn't see. "Meet me back here by five."

"Clorissa! You're supposed to stay with me until I groom Giana!" By the time Dani had pulled her cap off, her cousin had disappeared. Dani didn't really mind. She should have expected Clorissa to go off with her friends.

First thing in the gate, Dani flipped her baseball cap around backwards, bought a hot dog, and then hurried to see the goats. She'd find Carl and the horses later. Dani knew where to find the goats by their sounds. Little pens held white goats, brown goats, and black goats, goats with floppy ears and goats with no ears at all. Seeing all the goats made Dani pleased, then sad.

Tyler should be here. He was cuter than any of them and probably smarter, too.

A laughing child's delighted scream caught Dani's attention. Off to the right side of the pens, Dani saw a goat pulling a cart. Inside the cart sat a very small child. Dani had never known a goat could pull a cart. For an instant, she wished she weren't so big.

"Last call for Junior Showmanship," a voice called over the loudspeaker. "To the ring, please."

Dani wandered over to the field to watch. Older children led their goats around a big circular pen. Dani grabbed the railing. She could do that! A judge inspected the goats one by one. Each goat had a leash around its neck. The owner made the goat stand, then run around the ring. The third goat refused to stand still. She tried to climb on the judge and nibble on her coat. Dani giggled. That would be Tyler.

Someone tapped Dani's shoulder. "Well now, miss, tell me about this goat for sale."

Dani turned so fast that a skinny woman in a suit had to hop away so the sign didn't hit her in the knees.

"Tyler!" Dani cried. Maybe the woman

wanted to buy him. Dani stepped closer. "He's nice. About this tall."

"Do you have papers on him?" The woman ducked her head to peer over her glasses that were set on the very tip of her nose.

"Papers?"

"Records of his breeding." The woman waved her glasses in the air with a flourish. "To prove that he is a purebred Toggen-burg."

Dani had heard Uncle Walter talking about Jen being purebred. "We've got papers on the mother," she answered. "Her name is Jen."

"What about the father?" With her glasses back on, the woman looked like a well-dressed pink owl.

"I don't know." Dani had never thought to ask about Tyler's father. "My uncle would know. Please buy Tyler."

The woman frowned, then pulled a tiny pad of paper out of her jacket pocket. "What's your phone number, young lady?"

Dani had to think for a moment even to remember that, she was so excited. "649-6087."

The woman tipped her head back to see

through her glasses on the tip of her nose as she wrote. "I'll call tomorrow. I'll come look at him if your uncle has papers." Still writing, the woman strode away. Dani almost expected her to fly.

"Thank you, ma'am!" Dani called. She made herself stand still until the owl woman moved out of sight. "Hurray!" Dani jumped as high as she could. She got tangled up in her signs and fell.

She sure hoped Tyler had papers!

13 Giana's Race

Triumphantly, Dani bought a giant cotton candy and then headed for the games area of the fairgrounds. Mom never let her have cotton candy, but Mom wasn't there.

After the ring toss and the softball throw, Dani ditched her signs in a corner by the gate. She walked past a puppet show. Then she found the horse stable by the smell. She liked the earthy smell of horses.

Carl sat on his giant tack box right in the middle of the row of horses. On one side of Giana was Chessy. On the other was old spotted Elmer. A woman was clipping the shaggy whiskers inside Elmer's ears. Giana looked nervous. Dani could see her pacing before she even got close. She probably didn't like all the strange horses or the closed-in stalls. "Carl!" Dani waved her arm.

"Hey, Wild Colt." Carl called. As he stood up, he pulled a brush and a handful of ribbons out of the tack box. "Want to braid Giana's tail? Make her mane fancy, too, if you want. Half an hour until race time. I just finished warming her up."

Dani shoved the ribbons into her pocket and the body brush under her arm. Then she crawled onto the top of the gate. The horse nickered and trotted over. Dani thought she was the prettiest horse with her brown coat and shiny white patches. She fed her apple chunks from her pocket. Dani knew she wasn't supposed to feed her before a race, but she thought a couple of nibbles might calm her. Luckily, Carl didn't notice.

Giana didn't feel like standing still. She kept walking away while Dani sat on the gate and tried to braid her tail. Finally, Dani held the tail and followed the horse around the dark stall. She braided in a yellow and a green ribbon.

In a soft voice, Dani told Giana that races didn't need to be scary. "Pretend you're Pegasus." Dani secured the bottom of the braid with a brown rubber band. "Carl?" She stood on the gate, facing out to the bright sun. "Who is going to ride her?" Dani could feel warm breath blowing her hair, so she knew Giana was standing over her. The horse rested her nose on Dani's shoulder.

"Who do you think?" Carl looked up from the bridle in his hands, then pointed to his own chest.

"You?" Dani exclaimed, bouncing on her tiptoes. Giana neighed as her head bobbled.

Carl snorted, too. "Think I'm too old?"

Dani flushed. She'd known Carl was skinny, but she'd never noticed before how little he was. His limp wouldn't matter on a horse.

"I ride them all except Sands," Carl explained. "We turn him over to a real jockey."

Dani felt even more excited about the race. Carl came into the stall and checked Giana's saddle and bridle. Dani tied one ribbon onto each of Carl's sleeves. Then she looked at Carl's watch. "Shouldn't we hurry?"

Whistling softly to Giana, Carl held onto the horse's reins and led her out of the stable. Dani skipped by his other side.

"These ribbons will help," Carl said as they headed onto the field. "Make her feel right proud."

At the side gate, Dani waved as Carl

swung himself onto Giana's back. The pair trotted off, and Dani knew they would use the last few minutes to warm up and concentrate.

On a whim, Dani raced around to the front gate and pulled two dollars and a few apple chunks out of her pocket to buy herself a ticket to the stands. The line seemed to take forever. She could hear the announcer talking about the Two-year-old Race.

Dani scrambled to the very top of the bleachers. Giana's ribbons made her easy to distinguish from the other horses in their starting gates. Carl hunched over Giana's back. Dani had an urge to tell everyone on the bleachers that she had been the one to tie those ribbons on his sleeve.

The gunshot cracked. "AND THEY'RE OFF!" the announcer yelled.

Giana galloped out into the lead. Dani couldn't believe it. "Go, Giana!" Three horses overtook her halfway around. "Catch them! Catch them!"

Dani liked to think the beribboned horse heard her familiar voice. Giana immediately moved past one of the horses. Right before the end, she stretched her legs and neck out like a rubber band. Giana took second by half a nose. "Hurray!" Dani yelled.

Pretty good for her first race. Carl had already told Dani he'd be real pleased with a third. He'd also said he would walk Giana until she was cool. Then he would load her up from the back of the field and take her straight home.

So Dani decided to try her luck again at the games. By five o'clock, she had won a three-foot-high stuffed giraffe at the softball throw. She had spent her entire allowance for two weeks. Dani bought another cotton candy. Right on time, she met Clorissa at the front gate.

"Hey, pink mouth," Clorissa called. Her laughing didn't bother Dani so much anymore. That was the way Clorissa talked. Besides, she knew Clorissa liked her most of the time.

Dani hugged her sign and her stuffed giraffe against her chest as she rode home in Clorissa's friend's car. In the rearview mirror, she caught a glimpse of herself still wearing her new green baseball cap . . . her wish cap from Uncle Walter. What a great gift!

Maybe Uncle Walter did like her, the

way he used to before she'd come to live here and that giant wall had grown up between them. Maybe he just showed his caring in a different way than her parents. Mom would never think to give her a baseball cap.

Dani remembered what Clorissa had said about getting Uncle Walter to laugh. She knew she couldn't laugh with him, but she could try to talk to him when she got home. Usually, she just left him alone. She could try to talk to him about his painting. Then she'd ask him whether Tyler had papers.

Dani hoped that the skinny owlish woman with glasses would buy Tyler. She closed her eyes and imagined what the goat's new home would look like. Tyler would have a barn and a giant pen with fancy climbing toys. One of the toys would be a circular ladder that rose all the way to the roof of the barn. The owl woman would sit on the roof with him and feed him oats covered with molasses three times a week.

Clorissa poked her in the shoulder. "Wake up, pest. We're home." Dani wished she wouldn't call her a pest around other people. They both thanked Clorissa's friend's mother. Then they relatched the gate and walked down the driveway.

"Tyler," Dani called, but he didn't come. That was odd. It wasn't hot enough for him to still be sleeping. Dani stuck her head in the barn. Jen and Willy stood *alone* in one corner. Suddenly, Dani felt ice cold all over. "Tyler!"

Uncle Walter came around the opposite side of the house. He looked upset, flustered.

"Where is Tyler?" Dani asked.

"Gone," he said softly. He didn't look at her.

"Gone?!" Dani's heart felt as though it had been kicked. All of her good thoughts about Uncle Walter disappeared. He must have given her the new cap so she wouldn't feel bad about losing Tyler! He had waited until she left and then taken him away. "You sold him already?!" she yelled.

"Don't you scream at me like that, young lady. I — "

He hadn't even denied selling him. "I'm not a lady!" Dani exploded. She leaped closer to Uncle Walter. "You promised you wouldn't sell Tyler until he was four months old!" Then she threw the new cap on the ground and stomped on the yellow brim with both feet.

Clorissa gasped. "Dani!"

"You promised!!" Dani screamed.

Uncle Walter grabbed her shoulders. He lifted her up into the air and shook her once. Dani stopped in mid-scream.

"Dani, listen to me. I didn't sell him! When I got home a bit ago, the gate was open," Uncle Walter said fiercely. "And Tyler was gone. Jen and Willy were in the barn, though I don't know why they didn't all three go together. I just finished checking the yard." Uncle Walter plunked her on the ground, hard. "Now let's go look for him, little miss. *Together*. You're the one who latched that gate this morning. Didn't you bother to hook the chain?"

14 Gone

Every step, Dani screamed inside. Yet she didn't make a single sound. Uncle Walter had picked her up and shaken her! He walked wordlessly beside her now, looking at his feet. They marched from neighbor to neighbor. At each house, Dani asked, "Have you seen a brown and white goat? About this size?" Between the homes, Dani remained silent. Yet she couldn't quiet her thoughts. . . . Why hadn't she hooked that chain? Where could Tyler have gone? What if a dog had torn him to pieces?

Dani felt so tired that her legs wanted to collapse. She'd been walking all day at the County Fair. She clutched her back pocket so she could feel her mother's latest letter. *Mom! Why can't you be here?* she cried inside. She had to bite her lips to keep from moaning as they trudged along the shortcut through the woods she and Tyler had walked together. Dani stumbled blindly over a root, and Uncle Walter caught her with one hand. She pulled away.

The afternoon was turning to dusk among the trees. "Dani," Uncle Walter whispered, but she ignored him.

Dani crawled under the barbed wire fence of the horse farm and tried to whistle to let the dog know it was her. She couldn't make the tiniest sound. Behind her, Uncle Walter stepped over the fence. Nelly bounded across the field and circled him, growling.

Instantly, Carl pulled the big dog away. How had he gotten there so fast? It was almost as if he'd been waiting. Dani looked right into her friend's eyes. They were brighter than usual. He must still be excited from the fair. She muttered, "Giana ran a good race."

"Go look, Dani," Carl replied.

"What?" Dani didn't understand. She couldn't seem to think clearly.

"Go on, girl," Carl insisted and pointed toward the horses. He turned and held out his hand to Uncle Walter.

Why had he been waiting? she wondered again. Then Dani felt as if a sun rose inside her like the dawning of a tiny sliver of hope. "Is . . . is Tyler here?"

Carl didn't answer. He let go of Uncle Walter's hand. "Well now, Benson, where's your drawing pad? Never seen you without it." Carl crossed his slender arms. "Your girl comes here often. Her goat has come a couple of times, too."

Uncle Walter glanced at Dani, startled.

"Nice kid." Carl chuckled. "Nice kids."

Dani had already started racing toward the horses' pens. Halfway across the field, she stumbled and fell so hard that she landed on her face. Dani scrambled to her feet and spit out the dust. She kept running. The horses shied nervously as she came near.

Dani forced herself to slow down. She tiptoed to the bay's paddock and peered through the railings, the palms of her hands suddenly sweaty. But Tyler wasn't there.

Old spotted Elmer swished his tail and arched his neck as he paced around the next paddock. Dani had never seen him so high spirited. Creeping forward, Dani held her breath and searched each corner. She felt as if an ocean wave were about to crash over her.

No little goat.

Where was he? "Tyler," Dani called, but

the word came out a whisper. The goat wasn't in the third pen with Giana. Dani patted her horse's nose as she hurried past. The ribbons still looked festive.

Tyler wasn't in the empty fourth paddock where Chessy lived, nor the fifth or sixth. Only one more chance. Dani crept right up to the final large isolated corral where Sands lived. She hadn't been this close to the big sandy-colored racehorse since that time he'd tried to bite her.

The racehorse was *alone*.

Dani felt the sting of tears behind her eyes.

Then Sands moved. Right behind him stood Tyler. Sands lowered his head. The giant racehorse and the tiny goat stood nose to nose.

"Tyler!" Dani found her voice at last.

The little goat bounded toward her, his tail and ears joyfully sticking straight up. He leaned his head out between the bottom two boards of the fence. Regardless of the danger, Dani crawled closer. The chocolate goat nibbled on her hand, then her ear as she hugged him. "Aw, Tyler." Dani scratched him under the neck with both hands. "I thought you were dead!" Dani

could feel the roughness of his hair against her fingers.

"When I came out after dinner, he was in there," Carl said behind her. Dani craned her head to look up at him. "Pretty special goat," Carl continued. "He must have crawled right under that bottom rung to get in with Sands, here."

"Or climbed over." Uncle Walter knelt beside Dani. "That goat's quite an acrobat." He gently rested two fingers on Dani's shoulder.

Dani squeezed his fingers. "Tyler is all right, Uncle Walter." She kept hold of his hand.

"Guess you were scared losing your goat like that," Carl said. Then he hesitated. "Uh . . ." Tyler pranced back to the horse, and Sands leaned down to nuzzle his side. Carl shuffled his feet. "Now, I don't suppose you would like to sell him?"

Dani leaped to her feet. Carl didn't seem to notice her shock. He went on talking. "I know the goat's your special pet. But Sands here gets awfully lonely. And — "

"But you don't want any more animals around here," Dani's voice rose. "That's why I never told you I was trying to find Tyler a home. I wanted one place . . ." Her word cracked. "I wanted one place where I could pretend that Tyler was going to be mine forever."

Carl flushed. He stuck his hands in his pockets.

Dani had never seen him look so uncomfortable. She took a breath, then tried to say matter-of-factly, "Won't Tyler smell if you keep him?"

"Now . . . there's something we can do about that. At least most of that." Carl raised his eyebrows at Uncle Walter. "But he won't sire any kids."

Dani didn't care about Tyler's babies. All that mattered was that Tyler would live.

"I'd love to sell him, Carl. *We'd* love to sell him!" She twisted around. "Uncle Walter?"

Her uncle put his hand on her arm. Since he was kneeling, he only came as high as her nose. Dani tugged on the collar of his shirt. All the tears she'd been holding inside for the last week burst loose. "Tyler isn't going to die. Tyler won't have to be sold for meat!" Dani knew she was screaming, but Uncle Walter didn't even flinch. "He isn't going to die!"

Her uncle pulled her close.

Dani rested her head on his shoulder. Relief flooded her, then sadness. "But Uncle Walter, I want to *keep* Tyler."

Her uncle spread the fingers of one hand across her back in a silent hug. "Can't have all your wishes, can you?" Uncle Walter spoke so only she would hear. "Dani, you helped find Tyler a home. That's almost a miracle. And that was your first wish, the one dream you really worked to make come true. Tyler never would have found his way here if you hadn't brought him to visit."

Dani couldn't stop sobbing. She could feel a wall crumbling inside, the wall that had been there all these months between her and her uncle. "I want to have all my wishes. I want Mom here, too. Uncle Walter, I still miss Mom." Then Dani said something she hadn't thought she would ever say out loud. "I feel like she's never going to come home."

When he finally spoke, Uncle Walter sounded different than she'd ever heard him. "You are so much like your mom sometimes. The way she was when she was a young girl. She would throw herself into everything. Like you, teaching Tyler to follow you. Taking him out of the yard. Hanging from that flimsy old gutter with a rope in your teeth."

Dani pulled away to look at him. He looked more full of feeling than she'd ever seen him.

"I don't know whether I ever would have had the courage to be an artist without her. Guess she taught me to dream." Uncle Walter poked Dani playfully in the stomach. "Your mom was a pretty pesky little sister. And she's a fine woman. Just like you'll be. You should be proud of her, winning that scholarship. That was one of *her* big wishes." He grinned. "Seems like a long time, but a year isn't forever. Your mom's coming back, you know."

"Are you sure?" Dani looked away. She rubbed her big toe in the dirt. Talking about this made her feel as if she were six years old again.

Uncle Walter lifted her chin with one finger. "Does your mom lie to you?"

Dani shook her head, still embarrassed.

"Then why would she be lying now? She's coming back." His voice lightened. "You may not be able to see her, Dani, but your mom's here. Like a shadow in a picture."

Startled, Dani looked straight into her uncle's intense hazel eyes. Mom *was* like a shadow. Dani received her words and a picture of her now and then. Mom wasn't here, but her love was around . . . as truly as if Dani could reach out and touch her.

Dani turned slowly to face Sands's paddock again. Carl was giving the horse water at the back of the pen. She stuck her hand through the fence, and Tyler came over to nibble on her fingers. Dani kept hold of Uncle Walter's arm with her other hand. The thick hair felt soft, cuddly. She leaned against him.

Her miracle had happened.

Then she remembered how she had

thrown that beautiful baseball hat on the ground and stomped on the brim. "Uncle Walter, thanks for the wish hat."

His arm tightened all the way around her. For a while, they stood silently, looking at the two animals. Then Uncle Walter said, "Seems like Tyler chose his own home."

Dani nodded. She stared into Tyler's soft brown eyes, exactly the same height as hers now. He had found a place where he would be useful, like Uncle Walter said farm animals had to be. And he'd even be close enough here at Racehorse Inn for her to visit sometimes.

Tyler wasn't going to die. That's what really mattered. Yet Dani felt her tears start to come again. He wouldn't ever be hers, after today. Dani's chest ached. She stroked the white stripe on his muzzle with one finger. "'Bye, Tyler."

Dani pulled free of Uncle Walter's arm. "Let's go." She walked across the field, but she kept her head turned over her shoulder toward Tyler. Uncle Walter strode beside her.

The goat jumped on the top railing of the paddock to watch her. That fence was almost as tall as her uncle. Tyler, the acrobat. It seemed to take forever to cross the field.

Wasn't he even going to follow her?

When Dani had almost reached the barbed wire, Tyler bleated loudly. He hopped down and raced after her. Dani ran, too. She met her goat in the middle of the yard and threw her arms around him. "Oh, Tyler!"

Carl came up behind her with a rope in his hand. Tenderly, Dani slipped it around Tyler's neck, then kissed him on the nose. Tyler twisted his head to nibble on the rope.

"How much do I owe you?" Carl asked.

Dani solemnly handed him the end of the rope. "He's yours. *I'll* pay Uncle Walter with my allowance if it takes all year. Just take good care of him. He likes oats covered with molasses."

Carl nodded silently. He looked at her as if he were trying to say something, something special. "I'll tie him for a few days, until he gets used to his new home. In a couple of weeks, you come visit him, you hear?"

Dani couldn't answer. Somehow she had to make herself walk away from Tyler a second time. She swallowed.

"Perhaps next month you could come every day after school," Carl continued. "I could sure use the help. Your first job, you know."

That was more than good enough to get Dani going. She couldn't manage to say thanks, but she nodded at Carl. She knew he understood.

Dani ran. When she reached Uncle Walter, they looked back together. Tyler had already turned to watch the horse. Dani knew he would be happy.

Still, she would miss Tyler . . . horribly. Dani crawled under the barbed wire and took a deep breath. It was beginning to be dark, and she was so tired. "Uncle Walter, can I have a piggyback ride?"

"A big girl like you?" Uncle Walter laughed, but he knelt down.

Uncle Walter's back felt good. Deep inside herself, Dani knew now that Uncle Walter liked her. He'd said that she was a lot like Mom had been, when she was a girl. And he *loved* Mom. Dani nestled against his soft shirt.

Halfway home, Uncle Walter made her walk. "Too dark to carry you."

Clorissa met them at the gate. Dani could only see the outline of her cousin's body with the house light behind her. "You didn't find Tyler?"

"Carl's got him," Dani said. "At Racehorse Inn."

After Uncle Walter explained, Clorissa exclaimed, "You mean the lucky twerp's going to be a mascot to a racehorse? He'll get to travel more than I do."

Dani wanted to crawl into her cubbyhole and go to sleep, but Uncle Walter insisted on leading her downstairs to his studio. She hadn't been allowed in there since that day she'd gone exploring. Clorissa followed. Uncle Walter opened the door and turned on the light. He didn't say a word.

New sketches covered the walls. Dani tried to focus. She was so exhausted. She moved close to the first one, then stepped quickly to the second.

Tyler!!!

In the first picture, Dani was kneeling in front of the shed, hugging Tyler. In the second, Tyler had smashed his face up against the kitchen window, peering in at them eating. Dani rushed to the next one. Tyler was still tiny, looking out over the edge of the wheelbarrow.

"Look at this one, pest," Clorissa cried.

Then she glanced at Uncle Walter and said, "I mean, look at this one, Dani."

Dani stepped to Clorissa's side. There she was . . . chasing both little goats and slipping in the mud in her school clothes. That one was a painting. "Uncle Walter, they're beautiful!" He must have spent hours, all summer, drawing these. And she had thought he hadn't ever noticed her. "Uncle Walter, you're going to be famous!" Dani exclaimed. "I know you are."

Uncle Walter chuckled, pleased. "Pick two of them, Dani. Any two you wish."

Clorissa turned to stare at her Dad, shocked. "You *never* give away the drawings you are working on!"

"Dani will let me share them with her for a month or two. Won't you, Dani?"

"Yes!" Dani cried. "I want this one." She pointed to the sketch of Tyler peering in the kitchen window. "And . . . this." There she was, hanging from the gutter with that rope in her teeth. Tyler was staring down at her, his ears straight out like a helicopter's propellers.

Dani yawned. She couldn't help it. She thought her mouth would split. On the easel by the window was another painting of Tyler on the very top of the shed roof.

"Time for bed." Uncle Walter led her out of the room. "Why don't you skip dinner, if you're not hungry? I'll make an extra big breakfast in the morning."

Dani walked up to her cubbyhole alone and crawled into bed. She didn't even change her clothes. "Thanks, Uncle Walter!" She yelled as loudly as she could.

"Good night," he called. He must be yelling, too, if she could hear him so clearly up here. It felt good to have her favorite uncle back again.

"Stop screaming!!" Clorissa exclaimed.

In the moonlight Dani could see her calendar. Maybe living here from now on wouldn't be so bad. Only five more months and twenty-nine days until Mom came home.